MAKE MINE A COWBOY
COWBOY DREAMIN' 1

Sandy Sullivan

D1608061

Erotic Romance

Secret Cravings Publishing
www.secretcravingspublishing.com

A Secret Cravings Publishing Book
Erotic Romance

Make Mine a Cowboy
Copyright © 2013 Sandy Sullivan
Print ISBN: 978-1-61885-879-5

Second E-book Publication: May 2013
First Print Publication: September 2013

Cover design by Dawné Dominique
Edited by Stephanie Balistreri
Proofread by Courtney Karmiller
All cover art and logo copyright © 2013 by Secret
Cravings Publishing

PUBLISHER
Secret Cravings Publishing
www.secretcravingspublishing.com

Dedication
For the cowboy lover is all of us!

MAKE MINE A COWBOY
COWBOY DREAMIN' 1

Sandy Sullivan
Copyright © 2013

Chapter One

"No, no, no, no!" Mesa Arraguso banged on the steering wheel of her rental car with both fists. The gas gauge read *E*. "I can't be out of gas! I'm in the middle of fucking nowhere." The sting of heat from the leather burned her fingertips. The stifling warmth rose exponentially inside the car without the air conditioning running. It was, after all, the middle of May in Bandera, Texas.

A rumble of thunder broke the stillness as she contemplated what to do. She'd taken a drive to clear her head and jumpstart her muse for her next book, not end up on the side of the road, out of gas, with no houses within several miles.

This was cowboy country. Hill Country in Texas boasted some of the biggest longhorn cattle spreads in the state. Several cattle mooed in the distance but she couldn't tell how close a house might be. At least cattle meant humans…somewhere.

Large banks of dark clouds continued to roll across the sky. Several huge raindrops hit her windshield with a loud *splat* before the sky opened up in a torrential downpour.

"Just fucking great. Now fate is going to throw me into a huge thunderstorm. Why? Because I was stupid enough to go for a drive by myself during a writers conference in San Antonio and I ended up out here in the middle of the country. Now, I'm stuck on the side of some dirt road, out of gas, and God only knows how far from the nearest house."

Lightning flashed, followed shortly by a loud crash of thunder. Mesa jumped. A shiver raced through her body as her heart clenched in fear. She hated thunderstorms.

Her cell phone beeped—the ominous sound of no cell phone coverage. *Great!*

She glanced out the window and saw water rushing under her car along a gulley she didn't realize she'd straddled when she stopped. "Shit. Flash flooding? I'm so screwed."

As the water began rising rapidly, she realized she needed to get the hell out of her car before it was washed away. In the distance she could make out several larger rocks. "If I can get on top of them, I should be safe from the rush. Of course, that means I'll be out in the rain getting soaked." Fear rose, threatening to choke her with the lump in her throat. She rubbed her arms trying to calm the chills while deciding what to do. She really didn't have much choice. Water ran in rivulets down the windshield. Lightning continued to flash and thunder rolled over the area. She sucked in a large breath as she bit her lip.

A moment later a *tap, tap, tap* on her window startled her out of her thoughts. She jumped and screamed as a face appeared near her door. Blue eyes with long lashes stared back beneath a black cowboy hat. Black hair ruffled slightly with the wind.

"Ma'am? Are you all right?"

"I'm fine."

"You need to get this car out of the water. You'll be washed away. It's rising fast."

"I can't. I'm out of gas."

"Open the door."

"Hell, no. Do I look crazy to you?" she asked, her voice shrill with terror.

"Trust me. If I were a serial killer, I wouldn't be out in this shit trying to find women to abduct. I'm going to help you, but you need to get out of the car first before we're both swept away."

Mesa bit her lip. Should she trust him?

"Ma'am?"

"All right." She eased open the door to find the water almost reached the bottom of the car. The cowboy pulled the door the rest of the way as she grabbed her purse.

"We have to hurry," he said, offering her a hand to help her from the car. "Let me help you. This water is rushing pretty fast."

A red horse stood patiently several feet away with its head down, riding out the storm the only way horses knew how. *A cowboy on a real horse out here in the middle of nowhere? Surely, it's safe. I mean serial killers don't ride horses, right?*

Her tennis shoes were soaked the moment she stepped into the rushing stream, chilling her feet even though the temperature outside today was a balmy ninety degrees. She shivered as the man pulled her from the car, but chalked it up to her cold toes rather than the broad chest, wide shoulders and trim hips of the cowboy in front of her.

Oompf!

"Sorry, ma'am," he said, setting her back from where she landed against his chest. "Let's get out of this downpour." He slammed the car door before he pulled her toward his horse. "You'll have to ride behind me."

"No problem."

His ass looked fabulous swinging up into the saddle. *What the hell? I'm checking him out like a piece of meat and the man is here saving my butt from drowning.*

"Ma'am?" he asked, holding out his hand so he could help her behind the saddle.

"Oh, yeah right. Thanks." She swung up behind him and grabbed his waist like a drowning victim in the middle of a raging surf. "Sorry."

"No problem. You need to hang on. I don't want to dump you off the back."

"I'm sorry you're getting wet because of me."

"I was wet before I found you. I've been ridin' fences in between the downpours."

The horse sidestepped to the right. A squeal broke from her lips. "Sorry."

"You don't have to apologize, ma'am. I shoulda asked if you were okay on horseback."

As the horse continued forward she caught the rhythm of its walk and relaxed into the gait. "My name is Mesa."

"Excuse me?"

"Mesa is my name. I feel like some fifty-year-old woman with you calling me ma'am."

"Sorry. Habit."

"I can imagine."

"It's nice to meet you, Mesa. I'm Joel."

"Hi, Joel. Do you live around here?" she asked, liking the feel of his firm chest beneath her fingertips until she let them slip down to wrap around his waist. The urge to run her hands along the ridges under his wet shirt overwhelmed her, sending tingles up her arms. She could feel the ripped abdomen beneath her palms.

"A few miles up the road. My family owns a ranch on the ridge."

The man knew his way around horses from the way he sat comfortably in the saddle riding the animal's gait like he was born to it.

Well duh, Mesa.

The rain had moved off, only pelting them now and then with big, fat drops. The smell of wet leather reached her nose and she wrinkled the bridge at the stench. Another smell permeated her senses. Cologne? She slowly inhaled, taking in the scent from his shirt. *Damn, he smells good.*

"What are you doin' out here on this back road?"

"I took a drive. I've been in San Antonio at a conference and I needed to clear my head."

He chuckled, a low, dry reverberation that made her sit up and take notice. Her nipples pebbled at the sound, sending frustration down her back. Could he feel the hard nubs rubbing against his solid back? *Probably, you dummy.* It had been way too long since she'd been with a man if just sitting close to one made her horny. The rear end of a horse wasn't the place to get hot and bothered.

The material of her shirt caught against her breasts. The rough fabric of her jeans chafed the inside of her thighs. The seam of her pants rubbed against her clit, turning her insides to mush. Never mind the clean, musky scent of the man squashed against her boobs.

"What kind of conference were you at?"

"A romance writer's conference."

"Romance writer?"

"Yes. I'm an author. I write romance novels."

"Oh."

She waited for him to ask what type of romance novels she wrote, but he didn't. Wasn't he interested? Maybe not. Really, how could she tell him she wrote about guys like him? Westerns. Cowboys. Riding off into the sunset with some hunky cowboy on horseback. It would be totally embarrassing to tell him, so maybe it would be a good thing he didn't ask. "Where are we headed, by the way?"

"My parents' place." He chuckled again. "We'll get you some warm, dry clothes to change into. If the car didn't get washed away, we'll get you some gas so you can make it back to San Antonio."

"Thank you. You don't know how much I appreciate you coming to my rescue."

"It's what cowboys do."

Oh, hell yeah, they do. Especially in my dreams.

They continued chatting about mundane things as they plodded along. The constant shift of the horse's rump made her realize how long it had been since she'd ridden. *How far was this place anyway?* "Joel?"

"Yeah."

"How much farther?"

"A mile or so."

"Hell."

"Somethin' wrong?"

"I'm gonna feel every step this horse took tomorrow."

A deep laugh started beneath her fingers and rumbled up his chest until it burst from his lips. "You are too much, Mesa."

"I'm glad I could make your day," she grumbled, a little put out by his laughter. "I haven't been on horseback in ages. My thighs are already screaming mercy." She felt his body quiver from laughter again. "How do you ride all day without dying?"

"I'm used to it. I ride all day everyday so it doesn't bother me."

"You live on a working ranch?"

"Yep. Longhorns and city folk."

"Huh?"

"We have what most folks call a dude ranch. We let people come and stay on the ranch. Do ranch work, ride horses…you know, play at bein' a cowboy for a while."

"Really? That sounds like fun."

"How long are you in town for?"

"The conference is over in a couple of days."

"So you're flyin' or drivin' home afterward?"

"Flying, yes."

He got quiet for several minutes as the horse continued to walk along under his expert guiding hand. "What kind of books do you write?"

There it was. "Westerns."

"Oh yeah? Like cowboys and Indians? Louie L'Amour type stuff?"

She shook her head and almost unseated herself from the back of the horse. A fistful of his shirt kept her in place. "No. Like cowboys and the love of their lives. I write erotic modern westerns."

"Interestin'."

The house came into view and she sighed in relief. She'd be able to get off the back of the horse shortly, but it also meant giving up sitting behind Joel and removing her hands from his magnificent chest.

As they rode into the yard, she could see what appeared to be a main house and several smaller cabins of some sort. She assumed this is where the guests stayed. A large corral sat in the back of the biggest building where several horses stood. A handful of cowboys hung around the front of the tack room.

One guy stepped forward, taking the reins of the horse as she slid off the left side. "Hey, Joel. Where'd you pick up a rider?"

"Behave yourselves," Joel answered, swinging down from his saddle. "This is a lady whose car stalled out near the north pasture line. Mesa, these are some of my brothers, Joseph, Jackson and Josh. Guys, this is Mesa."

"Howdy, ma'am," Joseph said, tipping his hat.

Wow, twins? "Do you all always call every woman ma'am?"

"Yes, ma'am," Jackson replied. "Our mama would skin our hides if we didn't."

"Well, call me Mesa, please. I feel old when you call me ma'am."

"So." Josh moved closer, taking her hand and slipping it through the crook in his elbow. "How did a beauty like you get stuck with Joel?"

"Uh…" she stammered slightly as she blushed from the attention.

"Enough, Joshua. I'm taking her into the house so Mom can help her into some dry clothes," Joel said, taking her hand from his brother and capturing it within the warmth of his own. Tingles started in her fingers and worked their way up her arm. She frowned at the sensation. Surely she wasn't attracted to Joel other than being grateful for his rescue? *Why the hell not? I fantasize about cowboys all the time. He's the finest specimen of a cowboy I've ever seen.*

"Don't mind them, Mesa. They're all bachelors. When a pretty woman gets within fifty feet of them, they can't help but drool and act like idiots."

He thinks I'm pretty? "Thank you for the compliment."

"It's true. Anyway, let's get you inside and dry."

"You don't have to do that. My clothes are almost dry now from the heat."

"I'm sure you could use something to drink and to at least dry your shoes. I can hear 'em squishing from here."

"True." She laughed as she wiggled her wet shoe. "I would be nice to put them in a dryer along with my socks. I'll probably get blisters."

"Mom will try to feed you too since it's almost supper time around here."

"I hope I'm not taking you from your chores. You said you were checking fences when you found me."

"It'll be fine," he said as they walked toward the large, house-like structure. "We don't work on any time schedule."

Built out of what appeared to be logs and flagstone, the house boasted three huge dormers, a porch the size of a football field stretching across its front, and huge, wooden doors on the side they were headed toward. Joel held the door as she made her way into the dining room. Several picnic tables lined the huge room. Each one gleamed from the sunlight now pouring in through the big windows. Rough wood paneling lined the walls with a brand burned into several boards—TR with a circle around it. Huh. Interesting. *I wonder what it stands for?*

"Thunder Ridge."

He read my mind?

"It's the brand our cattle wear too."

"It's really cool you have it burned into the wood on the walls."

The smell of cooking food floated to her nose. Her stomach growled impatiently when she realized she hadn't eaten since breakfast. Joel grinned and her heart flipped over in her chest. *Damn, he has a sexy smile.* He could probably melt butter with that grin.

With her hands still encased in the warmth of his, he tugged her along toward a room in the back. "Come on. We'll get you something dry to wear, put your shoes in the dryer, and get you some food." As they approached the back of the dining hall, she noticed a small office built into the back of the huge room. The woman taping away at the computer screen seemed oblivious to their presence until Joel said, "Mom?" Mesa could see where Joel got his black hair. The cascading length only added to the woman's stunning beauty.

"Hey baby." She glanced up with the same blue eyes that Joel had and stared. "What'cha got there?"

"I found her out on the road with her car stalled."

Indignation ruffled her ego, causing her back stiffened. They were making her sound like some lost puppy or something.

"Well, welcome to Thunder Ridge. I'm Nina Young. This here is my son, or one of them anyway." She held out her hand and when Mesa took it, she pumped it several times.

"Mesa Arraguso. I'm sorry to intrude. I don't want to make you feel like you're taking in a lost stray."

"Nonsense. No intrusion. We love company. It's why we run a dude ranch." Nina looked at her clothes and said, "Oh my. You're soaked, honey. Let's get you something dry to put on. You look about my size. I'm sure I have something that will fit." Nina shuffled her out of the office leaving Joel standing in the doorway. "Come with me."

Nina walked her through another huge room with an enormous fireplace standing from floor to ceiling and almost wall-to-wall. Large leather couches invited people to sit in front of a roaring fire, should there be one blazing away. Not today, though.

Mesa followed Nina toward the back of the room and down another long hallway with a door marked private. *Must be the family's quarters.*

"What on Earth were you doing out on a back road like ours?"

"Running out of gas."

"Oh my, really?"

"Yes. I took a drive and my GPS got lost. Did you know some of these roads aren't on the thing?"

Nina laughed. "Oh yes. Our road doesn't exist on most of them because it's on our land. We maintain it ourselves." Mesa continued to follow Nina toward a set of double doors at the end of the hall. "We should be able to find you something to wear. Would you like jeans or a dress?"

"Anything is fine. I really appreciate this."

The room looked rustic with its wood walls, large bed, and wooden dresser along the left wall. Paintings depicted different flower arrangements of pinks and purples, matching the floral comforter on the bed. A couple of good sized windows overlooked what appeared to be a garden with roses, lilacs, and several other species of flowers she didn't recognize.

"We'll get you something." Nina opened a door to the right, exposing a huge walk-in closet with rows of clothes hanging on each side. Everything was color coded with yellows together, blues together, and so on.

"Damn."

"I have a thing for clothes. My husband calls it an obsession." She shrugged. "What can I say, I love to shop, although most of this never gets worn since we live out here on the ranch. I'm usually in jeans." Nina grabbed a red sundress off the rack. "This should fit you. Plus, red would look fabulous on you with your black hair." With a tilt of her head, she looked Mesa over from head to toe. "Do you have Native American blood?"

"Yes. Somewhere in my past, anyway. I'm not sure how far back."

"Ah." Nina handed her the dress before she walked to the window to look out. "You're lucky to have received the thick, dark hair of your heritage like some of my sons did from me. I am a quarter Choctaw."

"I have no idea how much or what tribe my ancestors were. It's not talked about much in my family."

Nine turned back to face her with a stern look in her blue eyes. "You should be proud of your heritage no matter how little Indian blood runs through your veins. We are a proud people. I try to bestow on my sons the love of the tribal people."

"How many sons do you have? I've met four so far."

"I have nine. My wishes for a daughter were never answered, although I hope to have beautiful daughter-in-laws and lots of granddaughters when the time comes. I have one grandson already, from my oldest son's failed marriage, whom I adore, but it's not the same as having a granddaughter to spoil." Nina took her hands and spread them wide. "You would make a beautiful daughter-in-law."

"Wait a minute. I don't even live near here. I live in California."

"I'm joking, Mesa, although you are a beautiful young woman and any one of my sons would be proud to call you wife."

"I'm only here for a few days. No matchmaking while I'm here."

Nina laughed and tipped her chin toward the floor. "No matchmaking." She walked toward the door. "I'll leave you to change. If you bring your wet clothes and shoes down the hall, we'll get them washed and dried for you. The supper bell will be ringing soon. You will join us for dinner, won't you?"

"I would love to, Nina. Thank you for all you've done for me. You have a beautiful home. I wish I could stay longer to explore. It would make a great backdrop for one of my books."

"You're a writer?"

"Yes, ma'am." Mesa blushed, dropping her gaze to the dress in her hands.

"You must tell me all about it at dinner. I can't wait to hear what you write about." She opened the door. "I'll see you in a few minutes. Take your time. There are sandals at the bottom of the closet that might fit you temporarily until your shoes dry."

With a soft snick of the door, she was gone, leaving Mesa in the middle of the huge bedroom to contemplate the turn of events her day had taken. First she ran out of gas, and then was rescued by a handsome, melt your panties cowboy, and now she stood in the middle of a magnificent bedroom borrowing clothing from a woman so gorgeous she could stop traffic. Wow, what a day this turned out to be. She surely didn't think things like this happened to ordinary women like her. Adventures didn't come her way on a routine basis. She could count on one hand how many men she'd been out with her in lifetime. Slept with? That would only take a few fingers.

After she quickly slipped off her wet clothes and put on the red sundress, she smoothed the material over her hips. The dress fit perfectly. A pair of leather beaded sandals sat inside the closet. They looked like they would fit. Slipping her feet into the cool leather, she wasn't surprised to realize they too fit perfectly. Weird. Joel's mother wore the same sizes she did?

Not wanting to be late for dinner as she heard the clang of the dinner bell, she grabbed the clothes from the floor and opened the bedroom door. Joel stood on the other side with a wide grin, propped against the wall with his arms over his chest.

"Well now. Don't you look pretty?"

"Thank you, sir." She dipped a small curtsey.

"I'm here to show you where the washer and dryer are, and then escort you to supper since the crowd is already gathering."

"I'd appreciate it, since I don't know my way around the house."

He took the clothes from her arms before he grabbed her hand with his warm one. "This way."

Within moments, they had her clothes washing as her stomach growled again because of the mouthwatering smells coming from the dining room.

"Let's get you some food before you waste away to nothing," he said with a large grin. They headed back down the hall in the direction of the clanking utensils.

"Oh please. I'm plenty plump that I could miss a few meals."

"You are not plump. Rounded in all the right places, I'd say."

"Flatterer."

He stopped and glanced down at her with a serious look on his face. "Don't let my brothers ride roughshod over you, because they will. They're a bunch of men, after all."

"I think I can handle it."

"Don't be too sure. I'll jump in to protect you."

"Aw, thank you, Joel." She skimmed her free hand down his chest. "What a gentleman." *What the hell made me do that?*

Her reflex was to pull her hand back, but Joel grabbed it in his before she could. "You're a beautiful woman. Other than guests, which are normally families with young kids, we don't get a lot like you around here. Prepare to be overwhelmed."

He kissed her fingers before he let his grip slacken on her hand so she could pull it free. The zing that raced up her arm bothered her. Those things only happened in her novels, not in real life. "Um, okay."

As they rounded the doorway, the volume of noise increased tenfold. Several people either sat at the picnic tables chatting away or they were lined up at the serving area with plates in hand. One long table she hadn't noticed before took up an entire wall. When she did a double take she noticed nine people, eight men and Joel's mother, who sat there chatting while they waited for the others to be served. *Holy shit! How many freakin' brothers does he have again?*

"Eight. There are nine of us boys."

"Stop reading my mind."

"Sorry. I can tell by the look in your eyes what is running through your head. You have very expressive brown eyes." Joel tugged her hand and brought her to the spot where there were two empty seats. "Hey, ya'll. This is Mesa." A chorus of hellos echoed through the room, shushing the rest of the conversations going on around them. Joel quickly introduced the brothers around the table and that's when she noticed two more who looked like...ohmigod. *There are three of him?* Yes, you could tell they all were brothers by the similar features, but...

"We're triplets," he whispered next to her ear with a chuckle.

Ah, hell! One gorgeous hunk to tantalize my senses is enough, but nine of them? And two who look just like him? I'm so screwed!

Chapter Two

Joel thought she looked cute with her eyes wide. Most people were surprised when they realized he, Jason, and Joshua were identical triplets. "Let's get our plates," he said, as the group of men took their places at the serving line. "We all wait until the guests have been served before we get ours. Mom's orders."

"She's a wise woman."

"Yes, she is."

"She must be tough as nails to raise nine boys, especially with three of them all the same age."

"I'm sure it hasn't been easy, but Dad is a strong man too. Never took any guff from any of us boys."

"Where is your father?" she asked.

"He's in the barn I imagine. One of the mares is foaling. He likes to be there in case there are any problems."

"Now, that I would love to see."

He shook his head and laughed. For a woman who wrote about cowboys and ranch life, she sure didn't seem to have much hands-on-experience with it. "We'll head out to the barn after supper to see how it's coming. Maybe you'll get lucky."

"Thank you. This is sure turning into an interesting day. I can't believe my luck. At first I thought I had about run out of any kind of luck when my car ran out of gas, but you showed up and rescued me."

"Oh, by the way, Jeff and Jeremiah brought your car to the ranch while you changed clothes. You left your keys in the ignition so they gassed it up before they drove it back here."

The server slid a hamburger bun with a large burger patty on her plate. "Wow. You guys eat hearty around here."

"Wait until you taste it. Even though I live here, I never get tired of the food. They always seem to get just the right taste on everything."

Next came the condiments, a bag of chips, and pink lemonade. The perfect picnic type supper. He led Mesa back to two chairs at the family table, hoping his brothers would behave. She seemed like a lady...a beautiful one at that. Sure, he'd been with lots of beautiful women before. After all, the reputation around San Antonio, and Bandera especially, had the Young brothers as catchable material for the mothers of the town. They had land—a worthy commodity in the hill country. Sure they had the reputation of being playboys, but it made them all the more chaseable to women.

"What were you doing out in this neck of the woods, Mesa?" Joshua asked.

"Running out of gas in the middle of nowhere."

They all laughed as she blushed a pretty shade of pink. "Actually, I've been searching for inspiration."

"For?" Jeff questioned. As the oldest of the brothers, he always had a suspicious mind about strangers hanging around the area. There were too many accidents happening lately, accidents involving their cattle. They had to be careful. Too many of the neighboring ranches were being bought out by big corporations wanting the land for housing developments.

"Inspiration for my books. I'm a writer."

"What do you write?" Nina asked.

"Romance novels."

"Really? How very cool. I'm an avid reader of romance myself. Are you published?"

"Yes, ma'am. I have a pen name, though."

"Why don't you write under your own name? Mesa is a beautiful name and very different. I would think it would be a great pen name."

"I love my first name. My mother wanted something special for me when I was born. My father is Italian and my mother said she is Mexican with a little Indian blood. I write under Mesa West."

"You have the beautiful dark hair and sharp facial features of your ancestors, Mesa. Do not be ashamed of it."

"Thank you, Nina. You've made me very welcome in your home."

"You are welcome anytime. I hope you come and visit another time when you can stay longer."

"Actually, I'm in the area because of a writer's conference in San Antonio. If you have room here at the ranch, I'd love to stay a few days?"

"Of course we do. I have a special room in the main house you can have all to yourself."

"Which room, Mom? I'll make sure it's ready for her. I imagine she'll need to go back to town to get her clothes."

"Yes, I will. Thank you, Joel. You've been more than kind."

"So what kind of books do you write?" Jacob asked.

Mesa pressed her lips together as a deep blush stained her cheeks. Apparently, she thought it embarrassing to tell a bunch of cowboys she writes about them with sexy heroines. He would have to learn more about her writing while she stayed at the ranch. Having never read a romance novel, he really had no idea what they had in them.

"She writes about cowboys," Joel said, earning himself raised eyebrows from his brothers. He shrugged his shoulders as he put a potato chip in his mouth. "What? I already asked her."

"It's true. I write about cowboys in modern day and historical settings."

"How hot?" Nina questioned, sitting forward in her chair. "I love the erotic stories."

"Very hot," Mesa answered.

"If you have some with you, make sure to bring them back. I would love to read some of yours. Cowboys are right up my alley."

The boys laughed as the subject changed to other topics including the buyouts of the other ranches.

"The Mitchells are selling," his father said as he approached the table with a plate in hand.

"Mesa, this is my father, James Young. Dad, this is Mesa."

"It's nice to meet you, Mesa."

"You too, sir."

"Shit, seriously? They're selling?" Jeff cursed. "Excuse my language, Mom. Mesa. How many more are we gonna lose to these sharks?"

"I don't know, Jeff. They seem to be buying up the ranches who have been hit the hardest by the beef prices. The drought hasn't helped either. Feed is scarce in this country half the time anyway, but when it doesn't rain, it's worse."

"We've managed to stay ahead by doing the dude ranch thing, right, Dad?" Jonathan added to the conversation.

"So far, yes. We've had a great clientele of guests to keep things going, but the prices are hurting even us."

Joel knew their whole lives depended on this ranch. They couldn't lose it. But the developers driving the local ranchers out only spelled harder times for everyone. The hill country was home, had been since before he could walk. The five thousand acres encompassing Thunder Ridge Ranch would be their legacy. Each of them. They all had a stake in the place and as far as he knew, they all planned to stay and ranch their own small section deeded to each brother when they turned eighteen.

His parents bought the ranch when his mom had been carrying his younger brother, Jonathan. Little did she know there would be a total of nine before she finished. Now, she wanted daughter-in-laws.

He chuckled under his breath. Little did his mother know, none of them had any aspirations of a bride at the moment. She wouldn't care, though. Fixing them up with decent women had become her pastime these days.

The rest of the conversation around the table went back and forth between who might be going out tonight to the rain pushing through the area earlier. Even though flash flooding could be a constant worry, they needed the life-giving essence of the rain. The ground right now needed it badly.

"If you want to head back into town after supper to get your things, I'll make sure your room is ready."

"Thank you, Joel."

"If you're back in time, we're having a bonfire later out near the pit. Most of the guests will be there."

"Sounds like fun. I haven't been to a bonfire in ages."

"We'll get you countrified while you're here if it kills us, city girl."

Mesa laughed. The sound sent chills down his back as goose bumps spread across his arms. The soft tinkle of her laughter reverberated along his nerves before settling in his groin. Not good. Getting mixed up with a guest on the ranch always came back to bite a guy in the ass He'd caved into the urge once or twice, much to his regret and his brothers' enjoyment. Not to say he didn't get his shots in when they decided to play. "I can show you more of the ranch tomorrow so you can get some ideas of the life."

The fork disappeared between her plump lips. *God, I never thought watching someone eat was sexy before.* Her brown eyes sparkled in the overhead lighting of the dining hall. He shook his head. Thoughts of her in any kind of romantic situation would just lead to trouble.

"I would appreciate it. I have a vivid imagination but to have firsthand knowledge is priceless. Makes it much easier to describe scenes when you have information."

"Do you know horses?" he asked, pushing his empty plate back.

"A few. I don't have any of my own, but I've ridden before."

"We can do some ranch work tomorrow if you like. Ride fences and the like."

Her smile lit up the room like a beacon for wayward ships at sea.

"Awesome. I haven't been on a real working ranch before so this will be the best experience I could ask for."

"Joel, you've got roundup tomorrow," his dad interjected.

"Do you think it would be okay for Mesa to go with us?"

"If she doesn't mind watching you and your brothers branding. Castration might be a bit much for her to watch."

"Oh no, Mr. Young. I would love to watch!"

"Please, call me James."

"Very well, James. I think it would be a great experience for me to watch everything." Her excitement almost bubbled over like a boiling pot.

"It's smelly, dirty, nasty work. The boys can tell you."

The group murmured their agreement, but she wasn't to be dissuaded. If she wanted to watch branding, she'd watch branding, he decided. He was going to give her the full experience for the time she would be in his care.

Most of the guests had finished their meal and put their plates in the tub for the dirty dishes so the group of men picked up their plates too. Mesa followed with her own until she spied the chocolate mousse cake sitting on the side cupboard for the guests. "May I?"

"Of course. It's dessert for everyone. You'll really like it if you are a chocolate person. It's very rich, though." He grabbed two cups and headed back to the table. "These are my favorite."

As she spooned a little bite into her mouth, her eyes closed and she groaned. It was the sexiest thing he'd ever seen. His cock jumped to attention behind the fly of his jeans. *Fuck!* She looked like she might orgasm at any moment and he wanted nothing more than to see the same look on her face as he drove into her hot pussy.

He cleared his throat and swallowed hard past the lump. Her tongue slid over the surface of her lips, swiping at the bit of chocolate clinging to her bottom lip. He wanted to suck her tongue into his mouth and taste the decedent chocolate mixture on her lips for himself. The groan rumbling in his chest stopped at his lips. If he let it out, she'd know how much her little display turned him on. *I'm so screwed.*

"You okay, buddy?" Joshua slapped him on the back and grinned.

"Yeah. I'm fine."

She opened her eyes and he noticed they twinkled with mirth. Of course she knew what she did to him. Didn't every woman have the ability engrained in her psyche to torture a man until his balls turned blue?

"This is fabulous, Joel. I'm glad you suggested it. I've never tasted anything this good."

"Glad you like it," he squeaked. He cleared his throat as he blushed. His brothers laughed, as they filtered out of the room joking around and punching each other. *Damn them all.*

The dining room slowly cleared of guests, leaving her and Joel alone at the table.

"I guess I should get going so it doesn't take me long to get back. I hate driving in the dark on roads I don't know."

"Would you like me to go with you?"

"Would you?"

"Sure. You know, so you don't get lost coming back."

"True. I probably will. Of course, you'd have to come rescue me again."

"I'd rescue you anytime, darlin'."

She blushed and dropped her gaze to the table. Surely, she wasn't embarrassed by his attention? Women like her should be showered with it. Curvy, cute, and sexy, with a rack big enough to bury himself in, would get her lots of interest around these parts, especially from his brothers. They all liked curvy women.

"Is that a southern boy endearment you all use to get in women's pants?"

"Huh?"

"Darlin'."

"I use it for anyone I like, so it doesn't apply to just getting into a woman's jeans."

She took his hand between hers, stroking her finger over his knuckles. The sensation reminded him of what she could do to his cock if he could get far enough with her. She'd only be there a few days. Maybe she'd be interested in some wild sex.

"Sorry. I didn't mean to insult you. I use it a lot for my characters. I'm curious if I'm doing it right is all."

"It is an endearment southern men commonly use, I guess. I never noticed before."

"Do you mind if I write all this down? It's great to have someone I can base characters off of now that I've met a real cowboy."

"You never met a real cowboy before?"

"Well some, yes, but not one who works on a ranch or lives the life every day. This is great!" She scrambled to her feet dragging him up with her. "We should go if we're going to get back."

"I need to let my parents know I'm leaving with you."

"All right. I'll meet you outside by the car. Jeremiah slipped me the keys at dinner."

As she headed down the middle of the room toward the door, he couldn't help but notice her cute little ass. His mother's sundress molded to her like a second skin, emphasizing the round curve of her backside. Her long legs would look good wrapped around his hips.

"Damn, I need to get my head out of the gutter. She's a guest. We don't fuck guests." He shook his head to clear the lingering thoughts as he headed to the ranch office.

"Mom, I'm going to town with Mesa to get her stuff."

"How sweet of you, Joel. I'm sure she'll appreciate the company. It is a forty-five minute drive back to San Antonio."

"I'm afraid she'd get lost coming back."

His mom looked at him with an arched eyebrow. "Are you sure it's not just to spend more time with her? She's an interesting young woman."

"She's a guest, Mom."

"I know. You boys don't mess with guests, no matter how beautiful they are."

"That's right. It's your rule." *Never mind the two times before. Mom would kill me if she knew.*

"It hasn't been a problem for you…until now."

"No problem."

"Are you sure? I think you're trying to convince yourself more than me." She stood up and wrapped her arms around his shoulders. "Son, if you're interested in Mesa, go after her. There is nothing wrong with finding the right woman in a strange circumstance. God has a way of bringing us together with our soul mate."

"Soul mate? Mom, I'm only thinking of fucking her for a few days, not marrying her."

"You never know. She might get under your skin so fast you won't know what hit you. Love works in mysterious ways sometimes."

"Stop trying to get us married off so you can have daughter-in-laws. I'm only twenty-eight."

"Plenty old enough to have a family of your own. You're all stubborn mules when it comes to women."

"No, none of us have found the one. I personally won't settle for anything less."

"Good for you, Joel. I don't want any of my sons to settle for less. Y'all need to hurry the hell up with this woman thing though."

Joel rolled his eyes. After a big hug, he stepped back and kissed her on the cheek. "I love you, Mom, but I'll find the right girl someday. Don't rush me."

"Rush you, hell! It's time all of you settle down. Especially, Jeff, Jackson, and Jacob. They're all in their thirties."

"Then go bug them. I know Jacob had a hot date with a girl from town last night. He didn't get home until early this morning."

"I'm worried about him. He's been drinking a lot lately."

"I know. I've tried talking to him about it, but he just tells me to butt out. He doesn't think he has a problem." The sadness on his mom's face hurt his heart. He knew she wanted the best for all of them. "It'll work itself out."

"He needs to get his ass kicked. Maybe that'll straighten him out."

"I don't know. Only if it's by a woman. I better go. Mesa is waiting by the car. We'll be back in a couple of hours."

"No problem. We're doing the bonfire tonight."

"I know. I already told Mesa about it. She's excited. She wants to see the foal being born, too, but I'm not sure of the mother's timeframe. I don't know whether she'd want me to wake her up in the middle of the night."

"She probably would want you to, but you need to get going. Don't keep the lady waiting." Nina grinned like she had a secret. His mother was playing matchmaker again, and this time he was the target.

Chapter Three

Mesa stood near the car waiting for Joel to emerge from the house. The whole ranch was beautiful. She couldn't seem to look quick enough to take it all in. The house, the barn, the cabins, the cowboys…Good Lord, the whole thing overloaded her cowboy sucking brain.

She frowned. That wasn't a good comparison for this particular situation. Not like she had an aversion to sucking anyone, especially if it included Joel. Her whole chest expanded with a deep sigh. Getting involved with anyone right now wouldn't be good. Her life included her apartment in Los Angeles, her cat, Tigger, and no boyfriend in sight. Even if she only wanted a quick fling, he wouldn't be the right guy to do it with. His charming good looks, cowboy manners, gentlemanly behavior, and nice ass in those jeans made him hard to resist, though.

Joel stepped out the door of the main house and headed in her direction. The wide chest, bulging biceps, and trim hips made her panties wet. She could easily fashion one of her characters to look like him. The dark hair curling slightly by his ears and around his neck, the sparkling blue eyes, the trim, sensuous lips she wanted to kiss with everything inside her. All of it made her body sit up and take notice of the hot man coming closer.

"Ready?"

"Yep," she said, opening her door. "You know, you don't have to go with me. I think I can find my way back by myself."

"I doubt it with these roads at night. Besides, you can tell me more about your writing while you drive."

She slid behind the wheel before she buckled her seatbelt. "You don't want to hear about my writing do you?" The car turned over with a twist of the key.

"Sure," he said, buckling his own seatbelt. "It sounds interesting."

As she backed out of the spot, she replied, "It's not very interesting, really."

"Why don't you let me be the judge of that? I've never met an author before." He pushed the seat back to accommodate his long legs. "So, explain to me what you write."

"I told you. I write cowboys."

"I got that part, but you said they weren't like westerns, really."

Heat crawled up her neck, splashing red across her cheeks.

"Are you blushing, Mesa?"

"Yes. You're teasing me, Joel." Her hands gripped the steering wheel tighter.

"No, I'm not. I really want to know what you write."

She inhaled through her nose, blowing it out through her mouth in a rush. "All right. I write erotic cowboy stories."

"Erotic?"

"Romance. The guy and the girl meet, they have some kind of conflict, they split up, and then they resolve things to get back together. In between, there is lots and lots of hot sex."

"Oh. Sounds fun."

"They think so, I'm sure. They certainly don't argue with me when I'm writing it."

"These people talk to you?"

"Of course they do. They tell me their story. I just write it down." She glanced at Joel. "I'm not crazy."

"Okay."

"You don't understand. The characters are like voices in my head."

"Okay."

"Stop it."

"No, really. It's fine. Just let me out here. I'll get a ride back to the house." He laughed at the sour look on her face as she scrunched up her nose. "I'm kidding, Mesa. I think it's good you write books."

"You don't think I'm nuts?"

"No. We all have our little quirks."

Quirks? "Authors are a bit over the top sometimes."

"I wouldn't know. You're the first one I've met, but if they are all pretty like you, then I don't mind."

"I'm not pretty."

"Sure you are. I like my women curvy, and you have just the right amount of curves."

"I'm not your woman." With a flip of her hair over her shoulder, she concentrated on the road in front of the car. Texas junipers sped by the windows in the fading daylight. More longhorn cattle dotted the landscape. Blacktop stretched in front of the car for miles. She knew she'd been driving away from the main road for a while before she'd run out of gas.

"Don't get testy. It's a compliment."

He shifted in the seat, bringing her awareness of him into sharp view. *Damn.*

"Do you not get complimented often? You should, you know."

"Not much, I guess." She shrugged. The sunlight had begun to wane, creating long shadows in the scenery. Rocks of all shapes and sizes sprouted from hard ground. She'd have to ask Joel what kind they were so she could be accurate in her description, should she use it in a book. Inspiration flowed, abound in her imagination since she met him. The surroundings of the ranch, his brothers, him, all of them sparked something in her she'd been afraid had died over the last year. Her writing had suffered—badly. Yes, she had a few best sellers, but her last book flopped. The next one needed to be stellar to bring back her fans.

The breakup with her longtime boyfriend, Kurt, hadn't helped matters, but she couldn't fault him. The decision to call off their relationship came from her. He hadn't liked it, but they parted on friendly terms. Their sex life fizzled out some time ago with her need to explore. She wanted more and Kurt had been satisfied with missionary position. No fun. No excitement. Nothing. What would sex with Joel be like?

"Do you write full time?"

His question brought her mind back to their conversation. Thinking about sex with Joel wasn't where she needed to be. Well maybe it was, but she couldn't act on it even though it had been a while since she'd been between the sheets with anyone. "Yes. It keeps me plenty busy."

"I imagine it kind of makes you a hermit, though. Sitting in front of your desk all the time."

"I guess. I don't go out much."

"Where do you live when you aren't going to these conferences?"

"Los Angeles."

"In L.A. itself, or one of the suburbs?"

There he went, stretching out his long legs again. *Damn, the man looks good in a pair of jeans.* "A suburb. I have a small apartment with my cat."

"Ah. A catlady."

Her head whipped around as her gaze locked with his. Those intense blue eyes stared back until she focused on the road again. "I only have one. I don't consider myself a catlady."

"Boy, you're testy. I didn't mean anything by it. I like cats."

"Do you have pets, other than your horse?"

"A horse isn't a pet. It's a working animal. Something required for my job."

She raised a hand and said, "Sorry. I think of horses as pets. They can be big babies."

"Ours aren't pets."

"But you love him, don't you?"

"Yeah. He's my buddy."

"Then he's your pet."

Joel laughed. "All right. I'll give you that. He's my pet. I've had him since I was young. My parents got him for me on my thirteenth birthday."

"Did your brothers get one, too?"

"Yeah. We all three got our own. Before, we would ride one of the stable horses. Jet is my horse."

"Jet? But he's red."

"I know. He fit the name 'cause he's quick. He's a cutting horse."

"You don't mind if I pick your brain while I stay with your family, do you? I'm realizing even though I write about cowboys, horses, bullriders, and all things western, I don't know everything I should to make my books authentic."

"Sure. I don't mind."

She glanced his way and smiled. "Have you ever ridden a bull?"

"A few times, yes. In high school, mostly. We all did those crazy-ass things during our younger years."

"You make yourself out to be this old man. What are you? Twenty-five?"

"Twenty-eight, but when you're doing rodeo for a livin', it makes you old fast. Ever realize there aren't a lot of old rodeo guys? It's a hard life."

"Any of your brothers do professional rodeo?"

"Nah. We have too much work to do around the ranch."

"Oh."

"Ranchin' is a hard life too. Don't get me wrong." He wiped his palms on his pant legs. "We get up before dawn most days and don't get to bed until late."

"I'm sure you all have a normal party life though, right? I mean, all work and no play makes Joel a dull boy."

"We get around," he said with a crooked little grin on his lips.

She wanted to kiss it right off his mouth.

The lights of San Antonio came into view as more businesses sprouted up along the sides of the road.

"What hotel are you staying at?"

"The Marriott near the airport. The conference is being held there in the business suites and ballroom."

"How's the conference been?"

"Pretty boring, actually. I was hoping for more reader interaction, but it's been mostly panels and such. There is a book signing tomorrow, but I think I'll skip it for the research the ranch offers me." She pulled down the road toward the hotel. The Marriott stood five stories high and encompassed the whole block. Concrete walls and steel framed windows, painted a bright yellow with white trim, outlined the hotel. Native bushes lined the walkways. She pulled into a space and shut off the car. "Do you want to wait here? I don't have much to repack."

"I can help you bring the stuff down if you like."

Hmm...a sexy man in a hotel room with a bed? So not a good idea. "Why don't you wait in the car? It'll only take me a minute."

"Okay. If you're sure. I came to help, you know."

"Yeah, but you don't need to see all my underwear and stuff strung all over the room."

He laughed a deep, throaty laugh that made her toes curl. "Fine. I'll stay in the car."

"Great. Be right back."

After she slipped out of the car, she shut the door and hurried toward the side door of the hotel. Luckily, her room was on the second floor, so it wouldn't take much to get her big suitcase and her computer bag down to the car. She really didn't want Joel seeing all her makeup, toiletries, and personal unmentionables. It seemed weird to have a guy in her room, especially since she'd only known him a few hours.

The door lock beeped open as she slid the keycard into the slot. When she pushed the door, the darkness of the room surrounded her for a few moments until she flicked the lights on with a press of the button on the wall. She grabbed her suitcase from the closet and quickly folded her clothes to pack back in the bag. *Shampoo, conditioner, makeup bag. I think I got it all.*

She grabbed her computer and slid it into the case. *That didn't take long.* She glanced around the room to make sure she had everything as she pulled up the roller bar on the suitcase. The conference had included her hotel room so she would be losing the money there, but the chance for front row seats to a real ranch setting would be worth it in the long run. Her book would be authentic and her hero would be to die for!

* * * *

Joel checked the reflection in the side mirror of the car. He could clearly see the door Mesa disappeared through in the glass. *What to make of her?* When he'd found her stranded in her car, he wasn't sure she had a brain cell in her pretty head. Who would take a drive out into the middle of nowhere without enough gas to get back? But while he chatted with her, he realized she actually was a very intelligent woman with a big heart. *She sure is beautiful with all of her long, dark hair and brown eyes.*

He checked his watch. She'd been in there for several minutes. *What the hell is taking so long?*

Tap, tap, tap.

Joel turned his head to see a security guard tapping on the window with his flashlight.

"Can I help you?" he said, after he rolled the window down.

"Can I ask what you're doing sitting in this car?"

"I'm waiting for a friend to come out. She's getting her stuff."

"She's checking out?"

"Yes."

"Why didn't you go in and help her?"

"She asked me not to. Come on, man. I'm just sitting here."

"In a guarded parking lot of a nice hotel. How do I know you aren't casing cars to break into?"

"Do I look like a thief? I'm sitting here in muddy jeans, cowboy boots, and a T-shirt."

"Step out of the car please."

"Are you a cop?"

"Yeah, I am."

Joel glanced at the man's shirt and noticed the San Antonio police badge. *Shit.* This is all he needed. Trouble with a capital T. He pushed open the car door and stepped out. His six-foot-four frame towered over the cop, but he didn't try to intimidate the guy. *Be nice to the policeman, Joel.* He heard his mother's voice in his head as clearly as if she were standing next to him. After all, the man had a gun.

"What's going on here?"

Mesa skidded to haul next to him with her suitcase dragging behind her.

"Our friend here thinks I'm casing cars."

"He is not, officer." She tapped her chest with her finger. "He's with me. I came to check out and get my things before I headed back to his house."

"His house?" the cop asked with a raised eyebrow.

Great. Now the guy thinks I'm soliciting or something. Shit. He stuffed his hands in the front pocket of his jeans. "It's not like that, officer. My family owns a dude ranch out in Bandera. She's a guest. I came with her to get her things so she wouldn't get lost driving back out there since it's dark now."

"Do you have your check out paperwork?"

"Not yet. I brought my suitcase out here first to put into the car before I walked back into the front desk."

"Put your things in the car then and we can all walk in together."

"Seriously? This is ridiculous," she snapped, hitting the trunk latch on her key fob. She slid the suitcase in the back before she slammed the hatch with a loud bang.

Joel walked behind her with the cop beside him. He couldn't help but notice how her ass jiggled a little as she stomped her feet. The girl had a temper, it seemed. He liked girls with enough gumption to stand up for themselves.

They walked in through the sliding doors. The desk stood off to the left with large plants flanking either side. Mesa had her dander up now. She slapped her hand down on the counter and snapped, "Tell this idiot I am a guest at this hotel and I don't appreciate my *guest* being harassed in your parking lot."

"And you are?"

"Mesa Arraguso. I'm here with the writer's conference and I'm checking out." She slid her keycard across the counter. "My room is 2103."

"Of course, ma'am." The guy tapped on a few keys of the computer. "You do realize there won't be any refund on your hotel stay because of the special rate and..."

"Yes, I know. Just check me out while I deal with this idiot." She stomped back to where he and the cop were standing. "Now do you believe us? We weren't giving you a line of shit, officer. What we told you was the truth."

"I'm sorry, ma'am, but we've had a rash of car break-ins around the area and your friend here looked suspicious when he kept checking the doors."

"I kept looking for her. Nothing more."

"I'm sorry but you have to understand, we are only protecting the hotel guests." At least the man looked sheepish. "I didn't mean to harass you."

"Then I suggest you go out there and find whoever is really breaking into these cars. It's not my friend."

"No harm done, Mesa. Really. He's doing his job."

"Believe me, I know how these guys work. I deal with the same crap in Los Angeles with the police out there. Everyone is guilty until proven innocent, not the other way around." The cop tipped his hat before he walked out the doors. Mesa huffed out a sigh. "Really, he should have been more apologetic. I hate being harassed like I'm some kind of criminal."

"It's fine. I get into trouble with the police sometimes in Bandera. Luckily, they all know us. They don't here in San Antonio." He shrugged. "I didn't give him my name or he might have recognized me. I don't like throwing names around, you know?"

"Yeah. I appreciate you standing up to him, though."

"I didn't do anything."

"Ms. Arraguso? Here is your receipt. Thank you for staying with us."

"I appreciate it. I'll keep this hotel in mind should I have need for a room in San Antonio again. Thank you."

Joel grabbed her hand as they walked outside. Knowing there were people out casing the cars in the lot didn't sit well with him. He had a permit to carry a gun, which he did in his truck, but not in someone else's car. Bandera didn't have these kinds of problems. The small town kept to themselves most of the time. To each his own. They took care of each other with their small police force and didn't have much trouble in the way of things in San Antonio. The bigger city had a lot more issues.

"Are you okay?"

"Yeah, why?"

"You're squeezing my hand kind of tight," she said, tugging on her limb although he didn't release her.

He kind of liked how her hand felt in his so he pulled her in tighter. "Sorry, darlin'. Knowing there are people possibly hanging out in the parking lot for nefarious reasons makes me nervous for you."

"Aw, how sweet. I'm fine though. I can take care of myself."

"Maybe, but as the man, I'm supposed to take care of you."

"Very chivalrous of you."

"It's the way my mom raised us. The men take care of the ladies." They'd reached the side of her car. Once she unlocked it, he opened the door for her, and then shut it behind her before going around to the passenger side.

"Do you always open doors?" she asked after he'd settled himself in the seat again.

"Yep."

"I didn't think men did those kinds of things anymore."

"Southern gentlemen do, but I don't know any other way to be, so there you have it."

"It's nice." She smiled and he relaxed.

"I'm just a simple, country boy."

"Perfect for what I'm needin'."

"And what might that be?"

Chapter Four

"Inspiration, Joel. For my next book."

"Ah." He quirked an eyebrow at her as she flushed in embarrassment from the little smile on his lips.

"Men," she whispered under her breath.

"What did you say?"

"Nothing."

They headed out of San Antonio on their way back to the ranch. Quiet surrounded them, so she flipped on the radio to a country music station and sat back in the seat, prepared for the long drive.

"Have you ever been married?" he asked, breaking into the low radio hum of the song playing. His voice reminded her of a sexy growl. She totally needed to use that in a book.

"What brought that on?"

"Just making conversation."

"No. I had a long-term boyfriend up until about six months ago."

"What happened?"

"We just grew apart, I guess. We'd been dating about three years." She glanced across the car, then back to the road. "What about you?"

"Nope. I haven't found the right girl yet. Of course, if Mom had her way, all of us boys would be married already and have a dozen kids each."

She laughed. It felt good with everything her life had turned into lately. Her career had gone into the toilet after her last book. Her love life sucked. "Why am

I not surprised? Nina reminds me of my mother. She's trying to marry me off, too. She was pretty upset about my breakup. More so than I was, I think."

"Only one of our family has been married before. Jeff. It broke up a few years ago."

"What happened?"

"Misha was a total ho bag. She tried getting half of us in bed with her. When she couldn't accomplish that, she went after the sheriff. She succeeded there." Joel rubbed his eyes with forefinger and thumb like he had a headache.

"I bet it's a bit awkward for Jeff then if he ever gets stopped by the guy."

"The two of them keep clear of each other. Jeff caught them in bed together. The guy was lucky Jeff wasn't armed at the time. Jeff just beat the shit out of the guy."

"He didn't press charges, did he?" she asked, her voice a slight pitch higher with worry. She liked his family even though she'd only met them a short time ago. They seemed close, like families should be. She loved her own parents, but they constantly seemed to be on her tail about one thing or another. When was she going to marry? What about children? Even though she was only twenty-five, shouldn't she be thinking about her future? Did she plan on writing novels for the rest of her life? She needed a day job to pay her bills. She'd been lucky. Her first novel took off three years ago and hit the NY Times Bestseller list, as did her second. Her third flopped...badly.

"No. Art knew better, even though he could have." He sighed and shifted in the seat. "Jeff loved her."

"I'm sorry for him then. It's not fair to put someone through the heartbreak. Just leave if you don't want to be married to them."

"She did want to be. She wanted the money and land she thought went with the Young name, she didn't want Jeff or their son."

"They managed to have a child? We wasn't at dinner."

"Yeah, purely by accident, I think. She hated being pregnant. Hated Jeff during the whole pregnancy. They fought constantly. She made everyone miserable while they were married. We were all thrilled when it broke up."

"No one noticed any of this before they got married?"

He shook his head. "You couldn't have told Jeff anything anyway. He never thought badly of her, even when the rest of us could totally see her flirting. He kept telling everyone she was being friendly."

Silence enveloped them for a minute as she contemplated how she would have felt had one of her brothers gone through the same thing with a spouse. She probably would have kicked the woman's ass for hurting her sibling. "I'm sorry for his pain."

"We all were. I hated seeing him hurting, but I'm glad he saw her for what she truly was. Unfortunately, because they have a child together, he still has to see her on occasion."

"Does he have custody?"

"Yeah. Mom and Dad made sure she didn't take off with their grandson. He's a cute three year old and gets into everything."

"I bet he's a total cowboy, like his uncles and dad."

"Yep. He has a set of boots, a cowboy hat, and the whole nine yards."

"I need to get a picture of him. I bet he's a doll."

"Looks like his dad." He cleared his throat. "Do you want to be there when the foal is born?"

"I'd love to."

"Even if it's in the middle of the night? It's very possible it'll come sometime tonight when you're asleep."

"I don't mind. Wake me up no matter what time it is. I've always wanted to see a foal come into the world."

"We can check out her progress when we get back to the ranch."

The time had flown. Before she knew it, they were pulling back up to the gate of the ranch. "See? I could have made it back without your directions."

"I see, but it does help having a GPS telling you where to go. They do get lost out here on the back roads."

"True." She laughed. "But I memorized some landmarks as we were headed into San Antonio so I'd be able to find most of the way back."

"I'm glad I went. It was great to sit and talk to you. You're an interesting woman, Mesa."

"Thank you." She scrunched up her nose as they pulled up in front of the hitching post. "I think."

He laughed and leaned over to kiss her cheek. Goose bumps rose on her arms when the smell of his cologne reached her nose. Of course, he had to wear her favorite scent, damn him.

"It was a compliment. We'll have to talk more tomorrow, but for now, let's get you settled in your room. Hopefully, you can get a few hours of sleep before the foal is born." She bit her lip. "What?"

"Can you get into the kitchen?"

"Sure. Why?"

"I'd love another one of those dessert things we had at dinner." She smiled hoping she could persuade him to sneak into the kitchen to swipe one of the decadent chocolates for her sweet tooth. She had a terrible one, especially right before bed. Ice cream usually calmed her cravings at home, but here, she needed to improvise, if only she could get Joel to go along.

The warm chuckle coming from his mouth made her smile. She liked his laugh. Hell, who was she kidding, she liked everything about him from the top of his sexy cowboy hat to the tip of his cowboy boots—the man had it all. Those lips made her want to kiss him into tomorrow. His chest made her want to bury herself against those muscles. She wondered what he'd look like without a shirt. Did he have chest hair? A lot? A little? She knew he had a six-pack. No cowboy who looked as good as he did, didn't have a six-pack, or sex-pack, as she liked to think about it. He had some of the prettiest blue eyes she'd ever seen on a man, along with eyelashes any woman would kill for. What would his hands feel like stroking her skin? Did he have a sexy happy trail? *God, I want to find out.* A heavy sigh escaped her lips.

"What?"

"Nothing. I just had a thought."

"Anything you'd like to share?"

"Really? I shouldn't because it would totally embarrass me."

"About me?"

Heat crawled up her neck as she blushed.

"Ah. It *was* about me."

"Totally."

"Share."

"Nope."

"Why not?"

"Because you don't need your ego stroked, I'm sure."

"Sure I do. Stroke me, baby."

She rolled her eyes and smiled. *I know he doesn't need a bigger head.* "All right. I totally pictured you without a shirt and I wanted to know if you had a little happy trail like most men with dark hair like yours do."

"Oh, you kinky girl, you."

He laughed. The rich, deep sound sent shivers down her back. *Damn, the man could turn me inside out and upside down.* She hadn't even known him very long. This wasn't good. How would she feel after being around him for several days? She hadn't quite decided how long she planned to stay at the ranch, but she knew it would be more than a day or two. The opportunity to have firsthand knowledge of cowboys, how they work, etc. wasn't something she wanted to pass up. "So?" she asked, her bravery waning now they were back at the ranch.

"Happy trail, huh? I've never heard anything referred to as that before. Explain what you mean."

"You know. The trail of hair usually linking chest hair to pubic hair." Her face flamed with heat. How did one discuss this kind of thing with a man?

"Oh that!" He laughed again. *The bastard.* "Yes, I have one. Wanna see?" He started unbuttoning his belt buckle as she shrieked.

"No! I mean not here."

"I'll show it to you any time you want."

"You're just teasing me now, Joel. It's not funny."

"I'm not teasing. I'm sure you've seen pictures of men nude before or in only underwear, right?"

"Well yes. Some have them and some don't. I'm curious about you since the hero in my head is turning out to look a lot like you."

"Aw, how sweet. I'm the hero in your next book?"

"It all depends on how the days I'm here at the ranch turn out."

"How do you want them to turn out?" He waggled his eyebrows and grinned.

"You're an impossible flirt."

"Yep."

"I bet every mama in this town turns their daughters' head away from you and your brothers when you hit Main Street. The whole lot of you are like this, aren't you?"

"Definitely, but the mamas are after every one of us to marry their daughters."

"Really?" His eyes crinkled at the corner as he glanced out the window.

"It looks like Dad is headed to the barn. Let's go see what's up."

"Oh. Great!"

She met him around the front of the car seconds later. He grabbed her hand again to help guide her to the barn he said, since darkness had fallen in an inky black curtain on the ranch. Soft country music wafted from the speakers next to the bonfire where several people sat around the crackling light. They would go there after the barn, she hoped. She hadn't been to a bonfire since summer camp approximately fifteen years before. S'mores? Hmm. She'd have to ask Joel if they had chocolate, marshmallows, and graham crackers, but then again, if she had her choice, she'd take the chocolate dessert they had at dinner. The smooth chocolate and whipped cream mixture was what chocolate dreams were made of.

"Careful. It's so dark you can hardly see your hand in front of your face. Without a flashlight, you could twist an ankle or something."

"But look at all the stars." She stopped so she could look up at the night sky. Billions of stars winked off and on lighting up the sky. "Look! A shooting star." She closed her eyes to make a wish though she couldn't believe she wished for a kiss.

"What did you wish for?"

"I can't tell you or it won't come true."

"Sure you can. I won't tell a soul. I promise."

"All right. I wished you would kiss me."

She could see the white of his teeth as he smiled. "Is that all?"

"Yes." The word came out in a soft whisper.

He stepped in front of her and slipped his hand along her cheek to bury his fingers in her hair. *God, it felt wonderful.* The slight tug on her scalp set her heart to racing a hundred miles a minute. A flutter started in her belly, spreading lower until she felt on fire from his touch. She closed her eyes as his warm breath spread across her lips. Her lips parted on a sigh, accepting the warmth of his mouth. His lips were soft, yet strangely unyielding, like he wanted to absorb her strength through her mouth. One of his hands rested on her hip, pulling her into the curve of his body. His chest felt hard beneath her hands. The soft brush of his tongue on her lips parted them to his invasion. She wanted this, needed to feel alive, needed to be a woman again.

A soft moan escaped her as he took the kiss deeper, bringing both of his hands up to cup her face.

The sound of wolf whistles brought her back to the present as she heard the catcalls from his brothers near the fire. Joel stepped back, breaking the kiss.

"Sorry."

"I'm not. It was totally worth it."

He laughed and grabbed her hand again as they continued on their way to check on the foal.

The barn came into view when they rounded the corner of the house. The large, two story structure with wide doors stood outlined by the moon in the background. A single, bare light bulb in the middle of the row of stalls reflected the black, wrought iron parts of the upper doors where the horses could stick their heads through. The barn was pretty fancy from what she knew about barns. Wood surrounded the bottoms of the stalls and each one had a sliding door. One off to the right stood open. She could see Joel's dad crouched on the floor next to the mare's head.

"How is she, Dad?"

"She's laboring pretty hard, son. I hope she foals soon." His big hands ran down the heaving sides of the mare. "I think the foal is pretty big for her, but she could drop it shortly."

"Do you mind if I stay and watch?" she asked.

"Oh, hi. I didn't see you there." He glanced back down to the mare. "You can stay as long as you like but it might be a while yet."

"I don't mind." She took out the ever-present notebook from her purse and jotted down information. She wanted to get the whole thing on paper for her next book. There's nothing like having a cowboy helping with a laboring horse to make the cowboy image stick in the reader's mind. She wrote more details, the position of the horse, the coloring of her coat, the rapid breaths, the concentration on Joel's father's face, the worry line along his forehead like laugh lines around his eyes and mouth. It mesmerized her how he ran his hands on the mare's stomach, calming her in the process. She could see the horse physically relax as he worked them down her side. She would have to ask more questions when all was said and done. Details like the gestation period for a horse, whether they could be ridden during pregnancy, how big a normal size foal is. All of this important information she needed...eventually. For now, the process looked worrisome for the two men.

Joel crouched down next to his father, balancing on the balls of his feet. "Want me to check her?"

"Sure. Maybe you can tell if things are progressing. I haven't checked her in a bit."

Joel stood and grabbed a long, plastic sleeve from the shelf outside the stall. Once he had it slipped on, covering his shirt to his armpit, he kneeled near the horse's rump and moved her tail out of the way. A lump formed in her throat as he slid his hand into the back of the horse.

"Appears it's in the right position," he said. "I can feel the hooves and they seem to be right side up. Its nose is right there, too. I think she'll deliver soon." He peeled off the sleeve and tossed it into a bucket in the corner.

"We'll just watch and wait then."

"Do horses normally deliver without complications?" she asked with her pen posed to write down his answer in detail.

"Yes," the older man answered. "The horse does all the work most of the time, although we do have to step in occasionally. There are times where they come nose first or with their hooves upside down, which can be a problem. With something like that, we call the vet."

"Fascinating." The horse grunted as her legs flailed for a few seconds. Mesa could see her side ripple with a contraction. Moments later, two tiny hooves appeared.

"Looks like it's time," Joel said, moving away from the horse.

With a gush of fluid, the foal made his entrance into the world. Slimy mucus hung from its body. The mare struggled to her feet, and then began licking the foal clean.

"Oh, it's beautiful!" Tears stung her eyes. She'd never witnessed anything so precious in her life. "Will it start nursing right away?"

"Usually within a couple of hours. The mother will clean it up first."

The baby stood on wobbly legs for a few seconds before it nuzzled against its mother seeking out her nipple. "Oh look! It's already trying to walk and feed. This has been fabulous. Thank you."

"We didn't do anything." Joel's father chuckled. "The horse did all the work."

"But you allowed me to witness this. I've got some great notes for my next book. I can't thank you enough."

"Our pleasure." Joel moved closer to her and slipped his arm around her shoulders. "I'm glad you got to watch the birth. She's the only one we have close to delivery."

She smiled, snuggling into his side to absorb his warmth. The wind seemed to have kicked up a bit, cooling down the heat of the day.

"How about we head to the fire so you can get your fill of that, too?"

"I'd love to."

"I'll check on her later, Dad, if you want me to."

"Thanks, Joel. I'll stay with her for a bit to make sure the foal is nursing. If you want to check her before you head to bed, I would appreciate it."

"Sure."

"Have fun by the fire. The weather seems to be cooling down with the wind kicking up."

"Yeah, you never know about Texas weather in April and May. It can be unpredictable."

Joel spun her around and headed toward the barn doors with his arm still around her shoulders. The weather had indeed cooled down, and goose bumps rose on her arms—though she wasn't sure if they were from the wind chill or the sexy cowboy next to her.

The flames rose into the night sky, stretching like fingers toward the inky blackness. Several people surrounded the warmth, absorbing the heat into their fingers by holding their hands or feet out toward the fire. Joel found them a carved out seat made from an old log. The bottom had been smoothed out of the cut log to make a great chair.

"Would you like a couple of marshmallows to roast?"

"Sure."

"I'll be right back." A large picnic table sat nearby with chocolate, marshmallows, and graham crackers for S'mores. "Do you want the whole fixin's?"

"No. Just the marshmallow is fine. If I try to make S'mores, they'll make me sick with all the sweetness. I love chocolate but too much doesn't like me, since I had the chocolate dessert earlier."

The rich sound of his laughter sent chills down her spine.

"A woman who can't handle chocolate. That's a first for me."

Heat rose up her neck in embarrassment. It was hard not being able to tolerate chocolate too much. She usually had to have a white cake with whipped cream frosting as a child because her stomach couldn't handle too much.

Joel returned to her side with a straight wire holder containing two prongs. With a marshmallow stuck on both ends, it would serve as their roasting stick. "Do like them barely roasted or black?"

"Sort of dark, but not too burnt."

He shook his head and handed her the stick. "Why don't you roast them and I'll eat whatever you fix? I don't care how they are roasted. I just like the sticky sweetness in my mouth."

Laughing, she shook her head. So much for being the difficult cowboy. He seemed almost too sweet to be true. She needed him to be a little more arrogant and self-centered to be the hero of her novel. Oh well. She could always tweak his personality a bit to make him difficult for the heroine to deal with. Ah, the job of a romance writer.

Within moments, the marshmallows caught fire and she lifted them toward her mouth to blow out the flames. Just right. Squishy but not burnt. "One for you and one for me," she said, holding out the stick so Joel could slide one of the fluffy things off the end of the metal contraption.

"Perfect." He stuck one between his full lips, grinning like a kid on Christmas.

Her body tingled in all the important places as he licked the sticky substance off his fingers. She wanted to lick him all right. Everywhere.

"Aren't you going to eat yours?" he asked, winking.

I'd like to eat something. "I'm letting it cool a bit."

The grin grew wider like he knew exactly what she had on her mind. *I wanted him a little more arrogant. I got it.*

"Have you always been such a ladies' man?"

"I've had my share of women."

"I bet you have."

"Jealous?"

She shrugged, trying to be nonchalant about the whole thing. "Nah. Just not surprised, is all. I bet all of your brothers are the same way. The women of Bandera and San Antonio better watch out when you all are on the prowl."

"When I find the one, I won't be prowling anymore."

The marshmallow melted on her tongue as she slid it between her lips. Joel's lips parted as one eyebrow arched over his left eye. Damn, he looked sexy as hell with the little smirk of a smile on his mouth. She wanted to kiss him again. Wanted to do other things with him. *Not a good idea.*

"Good?"

"Yes," she whispered, wondering whether she meant him or the marshmallow. The sticky sweetness on her fingers had her licking it off as she watched his eyes dilate in the firelight. He sure seemed like he might be a little into her. The whole thing seemed weird, though. Surely a guy like him wasn't attracted to a girl like her. She knew her hips were too wide and her butt seemed a bit too big for her liking. Getting guys like him to notice her didn't come with instructions. Popular wasn't an affliction she had growing up. She was the quiet, shy girl. Something she had to get over rather quickly as a writer, since she was in front of dozens of people at times, but she never quite managed to be outgoing with men.

Jason sauntered over. "Hey you two."

"Jason."

"Would you like more marshmallows, Mesa? You seemed to be enjoying them."

"Sure. Thanks."

Jason took her stick from her hand and headed back to the table.

"Don't get too close to him." The serious tone of Joel's voice had her on edge.

"Close?"

"I mean be careful."

"Why? He seems like a nice guy. You wouldn't warn me away from one of your own brothers, would you?"

"He's my brother, yes, and I love him but he likes to play with women."

"I don't understand," she said, sitting forward on her seat to hear him better.

Joel grasped her hand in his. "If you want the bad boy for your novel, he's your man. He's more into one-night stands than any of my other brothers. Women are like playthings for him. He doesn't get serious about women at all."

"You know, he does sound like the bad boy of the group."

"Well, we all are to some extent, but he seems like the worst. I don't know if he'll ever settle down."

"Why don't you tell me about each one in turn? Give me details of their lives, their personalities. You know. Those kinds of things. I can morph all of your personality traits into one kick-ass hero."

Jason returned with her marshmallow stick. "Here you go."

"Thanks."

"Don't listen to Joel about me. He's a bit biased because he's not as attractive as I am."

She laughed at his words. They were identical in most ways, especially looks. "You two are terrible to tease me like that."

The two men laughed. Jason sauntered back to his spot, flashing her a wicked grin and a wink from his seat several feet away.

"Okay. You want to know more about each of us. I'll start with Jeff. He's the eldest at thirty-four. I already told you he'd been married once before."

"Yes." She pulled her pen and paper out to jot down some notes.

"Jeff is Mom and Dad's pride and joy. The prodigal older son. He helps Dad run things around here. He's kind of bossy, but he's a good guy. We all hated when his marriage broke up because he really loved her. On the other hand, we were glad because she wasn't the right woman for him. I hated to see him so heartbroken. He's very adamant about running this place as a working cattle ranch. He didn't like when we went to accepting guests here to supplement the income. Sometimes I think he was born in the wrong time. He's cowboy to the bone. I hate to see the woman he really falls hard for because she better be country through and through to win his heart. He won't settle for some high rise, corporate type."

Mesa quickly wrote down Joel's description of his older brother along with a few notes on the woman who would turn out to be someone he could live the rest of his life with. As a romance author, she grinned. The hero didn't always fall in love with the woman he thought he would. She giggled a little.

"Jackson is the second eldest. He does what he has to do around here, but sometimes I think he hates playing the cowboy. He rides a motorcycle more than he does a horse. He has several tattoos, gets a bit rowdy when he drinks, but overall he's a great guy and good friend. He's saved my ass more than once in a bar fight."

"Do you fight often?"

"No. I try to be the peacekeeper more than anything. Jackson likes the ladies, too."

"Don't you all?"

Joel grinned. "Yeah, I guess so. The women seem really attracted to his bad boy persona, though. I think it's the tats."

"Could be."

"He's really a big teddy bear, though. I think he got more of Dad's personality whereas some of the rest of us are more like Mom. Jacob is third. He's thirty this year and is feeling every bit of it, I think. He's been drinking a lot lately. I'm not sure if he's debating his life—. Not that he would ever hurt himself or anything, but I wonder sometimes if he knows where his life is going. He's kind of quiet. More so than the rest of us. He just does his work around here and spends a lot of time in his room. Doing what, I'm not sure. He didn't do sports in school like most of us did. He's more the creative, artsy type."

"He sounds sweet."

Joel smile and shrugged. "Fourth is us triplets. Me, Jason, and Josh. You know about me. Josh, we're a little worried about. He's been drinking a lot lately, too I think he got his heart broken recently. He won't talk about it though. I've tried. We are very similar in looks, but our personalities are very different. At least to me, they are."

"Josh is a ladies' man, definitely."

"Yeah, but he's been down in the dumps lately. I hope whoever broke his heart was worth the pain he's going through now. I hate to see him like this. He's trying, but you can see the pain in his eyes if you look hard enough."

"It's never easy breaking up with someone you've been with for a long time even if it's a mutual breakup."

"True. I haven't been in a long-term relationship really, so I wouldn't know that kind of pain. I hope I never do."

She dropped her gaze to her paper for a moment and let his words sink in. Why didn't she feel pain over her breakup with her ex? She loved him, didn't she? Maybe not like she should have. The pain didn't seem to be there.

"And then there is Jason."

"You almost sound exasperated by him."

"He's an exasperating individual."

"How so?"

"He likes the ladies. Definitely. I think he's got several women on the string at the moment and I'm just waiting for the bubble to burst. If they found out about each other, it could sure make for some interesting fireworks in the neighborhood."

"Ah."

Joel scraped the toe of his boot in the dirt, digging up a small rock in the process. "This isn't the first time he's done this type of thing either. He's been caught before and almost got himself shot by one girl's father. He found Jason's ass hanging out the window of the daughter's room a few years ago. His truck still bears the bullet hole."

"Wow."

"I think my parents wish he would go in the military or something to straighten his ass out, but then they'd be totally worried he'd be in some combat zone and get his butt killed or something."

"I think your parents could handle it."

"I think my dad could, but I'm not sure about Mom. She loves having her sons around here."

"I'm sure she does. She's a very strong lady, though." Mesa tucked a stray piece of hair behind her ear.

"Yes, she is. I doubt Jason will do anything of the sort. Military lifestyle doesn't suit him, I don't think. He likes sleeping late, getting into trouble, and staying out all hours of the night. The discipline would do him good, but I doubt he'd do it."

"Trouble with a capital T."

Joel chuckled. "The fifth of us is Jonathan. He tries to be the cowboy Dad wanted in all of us, but he's not so much cut out for the life. He rides, but he's not as comfortable on a horse as the rest of us. He's more at home in front of a computer. He's a gamer."

"Nothing wrong with that. Computer programmers make good money."

"Yeah, but he doesn't get to do it much. I think Dad should let him take over the website and marketing for the ranch, but he hires out to someone else. Dad doesn't see the potential in Jonathan doing it. I do. I think he'd been great at it. If they send Jonathan to school so he could get some formal training, he'd be kick-ass at it. I don't think Jonathan has ever had a girlfriend. He's really shy."

She laughed. "I didn't think any of you were shy."

Joel grinned. "He really isn't when you get to know him. I think he feeds off the rest of us with our personalities. He kind of goes along with the bunch."

"I bet he's got a deeper personality than you give him credit for."

"Maybe." He lifted his gaze and glanced across the fire to where Jeremiah sat talking with a couple of the young women who were guests. "Jeremiah is the sixth in the bunch." Joel shrugged as he shifted on the seat. "How do I describe him? Hmm. He tends bar at the local club when he's not working the ranch. I don't think he cares so much for the ranch work. He likes doing financial stuff. He plays the stock market a lot. He's a very personable guy and gets along with just about everyone. See how he's talking to those girls?"

"Yeah."

"Most would think he's flirt. Trying to get one of them in bed with him, but he's not."

"No?"

"Nope. He just likes to talk to people. The numbers thing is really what he likes. I constantly see him with his nose buried in the newspaper or on the computer. Someday I expect him to be rich beyond all of us the way he plays with numbers. I'm not sure why he's here at the ranch except that he doesn't want to leave Mom and Dad. He'd be better off in New York or somewhere."

"Wow. Such a diverse group you have here." The notes on the group were getting longer and longer. How much more could she possibly need to develop the hero in her book? Maybe there needed to be an entire family.

"Then there is Joey or Joe. He's the baby of the family and boy do we all know it. He gets away with murder. I swear. Mom and Dad think he can do no wrong. Well, it looks like it from the rest of us boys' perspective anyway. He's the one in charge of the horses. He helps Dad buy and sell those for the Remuda and keeps us in a good supply of gentle to a little more rowdy for the experienced riders. We have a wide range of horses we keep on the property. Joe breaks most of the newer horses and he competes in bronc riding at the rodeo. I think he does some bull riding on the side, too although he doesn't want Mom to know about it and it's not professionally. One of these days, he's gonna break his neck, but it's what he loves. He's got the adrenaline junkie personality. Definitely attracts the buckle bunnies with his happy-go-lucky attitude. Woman in every town."

"Wow. You've got such a wide variety of personalities in your brothers. I've got five pages of notes on them."

"Good. I hope you get some great information while you're here."

"This is going to be awesome, Joel. Thank you for giving me the lowdown on everyone." She reached over and kissed him on the cheek.

"Would you like to go for a walk?"

"In the dark?"

"I grabbed a small flashlight while we were in the barn."

"Okay," she said, sliding her pen and notebook into her purse. She wasn't sure how much they could see in the dark, but she didn't want to call it a night quite yet. Being close to Joel ramped up the heat between them. Her body felt on fire as she shivered in the night air. It wasn't from being cold.

As they stood to make their way into the blackness surrounding the bonfire, one of his brothers called out, "Behave yourself, Joel. She's a guest."

"What's that all about?"

A shrug lifted both his shoulders as he laid his hand on the small of her back guiding her around the boulders and path rocks blocking their way. "Nothing really. We just have a don't mess with the guests policy."

"Oh?"

"Yeah. It's really to keep my brothers from coming onto some of the single women we get staying here, which doesn't happen a lot. We tend to meet more women in town. The ranch is packed most of the time with families."

"Does the no messing with the guests policy include me since you kissed me?" she asked, cuddling closer to his side. She really hoped the policy didn't apply to her. She wanted Joel to kiss her again.

Chapter Five

He stopped and looked down at her. "Technically, yes. I shouldn't have kissed you earlier. I'm sorry."

"Don't be. I wished for it. Remember?"

"Yeah, but…"

She pressed two fingers to his lips. "I wanted you to. It's not your fault. If your mother says anything, it was me, not you."

The warmth of his lips under her fingertips sent chills down her arms. He kissed her fingers, then her palm. Shivers raced down her back. Her heart sped up, threatening to jump from her chest.

Moonlight lit the path now that they were away from the fire. It also reflected the white of his teeth as he smiled. The wink he gave her did nothing to calm her out of control libido.

"I'll blame it all on you then."

"Great." He grabbed her hand to lead her down the path headed for the front of the house. Clouds raced across the face of the moon blocking the light at times, but giving everything an slight eerie silver glow.

He led her to the front of the main house where several rocking chairs and other assorted benches lined the porch in front of the windows. Light from the main room of the lodge spilled out onto the front lawn, but did nothing to cut the darkness beyond fifty feet. Joel took her shoulders in both of his hands as he pushed her down on one of the rockers. "I thought you might like to sit here for a bit and watch the clouds drift across the moon. It always seems kind of strange to me to watch with the outline of the trees beyond the light from the house."

"It is spooky out here."

The front door of the ranch house creaked open, but no one came out. She glanced at Joel, but he didn't seem to notice. *It was probably someone from inside who opened the door, and then changed their mind about coming outside.* She glanced through the window, but didn't see anyone near the door. *Okay, that's weird.*

"How long have you lived in Los Angeles?"

"All my life. My parents moved there before I was born."

"Do they still live there?"

"Sort of. They spend part of the year in Arizona." His profile intrigued her. The slope of his nose looked regal, except for the small bump near the bridge indicating he'd broken it at least once. His lashes were long, dark spikes any woman would give her eyeteeth to have. The black Stetson sat back on his head, framing the black curtain of his hair. He wore it longer than most guys, she noticed, almost to his shoulders.

"What?"

"Nothing, why?"

"You're staring at me." He smiled and winked.

"Sorry. I didn't mean to. I'm admiring your profile."

"Why?"

"I'm committing it to memory for a book cover. I want to take your picture before I leave." *Yeah, sounded like a good excuse to me. I certainly can't tell him I think he's hotter than Hades.*

"Oh?"

"Yeah. Preferably with your shirt off."

He laughed. The rich, deep sound made her pussy weep with need. *God, I want this man to make love to me. Make love, hell! I want him to fuck me six ways to Sunday.*

With a quick glance at his watch, he said, "How would you like to go into town? The bar there should be just starting to swing right about now."

"Sure. I haven't been out to a bar in quite a while."

"No?" He stood and held out a hand to help her to her feet.

"Nope."

"Well then you need to loosen up a bit. Have a few drinks. Dance."

"I can't dance."

He tucked her hand into the crook of his elbow as they walked back toward the parked cars behind the main house.

"Sure you can. Everyone can dance."

"I have two left feet. Trust me."

"Have you ever tried to two-step?"

"No."

"I'll teach you. It's easy. I'll lead, you follow. You'll have the hang of it in no time."

"I'll probably bruise your feet stepping on them."

"You can't be any worse than Willa Miller."

"Who?" She giggled as he opened the door to the biggest truck she'd seen in her life. White and huge with big mud tires.

"Willa Miller. She's been hanging out at the bars since she turned twenty-one. She's now fifty something, I think." Once he got around the front of the truck, he hopped inside and closed his own door. "She's got to be the worst dancer I've ever seen. Most of the guys tolerate her because she so sweet, but man she's hard on the toes." Her laugh turned into a snort. Joel roared with laughter as he turned over the engine. "You snort when you laugh."

"Only when I'm laughing really hard." She placed her hand over her nose and mouth trying to hide the sound. "It's not funny, Joel."

"Sure it is. I think it's cute." He grabbed her hand to lace their fingers together.

"You would." *What to make of this enigma named Joel?* He acted like he was attracted to her, but she didn't know whether to take him seriously or not. Could they have a fling for a few days while she stayed on the ranch? She could. Would he be willing? The attraction was definitely there on her part. She slowly pulled her hand out of his grasp to wrap her arms around herself. What to do?

"Are you cold? I can turn on the heater if you want."

"No. I'm fine. I got the shivers for a minute, is all." She rubbed her arms to calm the chills.

Within moments they pulled into a bustling bar in the center of Bandera. Tons of trucks sat in the parking lot, but very few cars. *Figures. Everyone drives a truck in cowboy country.*

Joel walked around the front of the truck to open her door. Such a gentleman, but then again, his mama raised him to be like that, especially around women. He opened the door and held out his hand to help her down from the twenty feet off the ground his truck stood— okay, maybe not that high.

"I should have dressed up more."

"You look great, Mesa. Besides, most of the women in here wear jeans and T-shirts."

"Maybe I'm overdressed then."

"I like you just the way you are."

"Thanks."

The doors to The Dusty Boot opened and closed several times as they made their way closer. She could hear the music playing loudly every time they opened. Several cowboys stood on the porch and called to Joel when they reached the doors. He waved back, but didn't stop to chat.

They walked inside only to be immediately swallowed up in the crowd of cowboy hats and rhinestones. A band played from a small stage near the back of the bar. A loud cowbell clanged causing her to jump. Joel put his lips near her ear. "The mechanical bull. They ring the bell when someone rides for eight seconds."

"Are you going on it?" she asked, breathing in his cologne. All man, cowboy, and musk. *God, he smells good.*

"If you will."

"Me?"

"Yep. I want to see those sexy hips swing with the back end of the bull."

Heat crept up her neck as she bit her lip to hide her smile. Sexy hips, huh. She almost felt giddy. He thought she had sexy hips. "Okay. I'll give it a go."

The smile he gave her could have set her panties on fire. She sniffed hoping she didn't smell smoke, because damn, he probably would melt the silk of her underwear.

"Hey baby." A beautiful blonde scooted close and pressed her size double D breasts against Joel side. "I've missed you. You haven't been around here much, Joel."

"No, I haven't."

"Wanna hang out? I'm free tonight and all yours."

"I'm with someone, Brandy."

"Oh yeah?"

"Yes. Brandy this is Mesa. Mesa, Brandy."

"Nice to meet you," Mesa said, glancing at the woman hoping she could hide her disdain. The blonde didn't even acknowledge her. *Well, so much for pleasantries.*

"I'll see you around, Brandy."

"Sure, cowboy. Call me."

"Uh, yeah."

Joel took Mesa's hand and wormed his way through the crowd toward the back of the bar. A large mechanical bull sat in the middle of a padded ring. Several people stood around the outside of the ring, laughing whenever someone climbed on and was tossed off on their ass.

Great. He wants me to get on that thing?

"Yes, I do," Joel said. "Climb on. You can do it."

Joel went back to pay the operator as she sucked in a ragged breath. *I can do this. With Joel watching, it'll be much more fun.* She grinned as she realized she could totally tease Joel at the same time. With a sexy swing of her hips, she approached the steel beast. She stuck her foot into the metal stirrup and swung her leg over the back of the bull. Adjusting herself toward the handhold, she tucked her dress between her thighs so she could save what little modesty she possessed, and then grinned like an idiot. Centered on the bull, she flung her left arm out and nodded to the operator to start the ride. Once the bull started bucking, she shifted her body in the sexiest motion she could as she glanced at Joel standing off to the side. He wolf-whistled, bringing a smile to her lips.

The music seemed to roll along her spine with each swing of the bull. Her left arm snapped back and forth as she rode for the full eight seconds and earned herself the cowbell ring. When she jumped off the back of the bull, Joel met her in the middle of the padded ring, swept her up in his arms, and planted a fat, juicy kiss on her mouth.

She lost the ability to think beyond his mouth on hers. Their tongues entwined, battling from her mouth to his and back. He lifted her up in his arms, holding her against his chest as she wrapped her arms around his neck.

Moments later, someone slapped him on the back and they broke apart as the guy jokingly told him to take it somewhere else.

She was so embarrassed she hid her face in his chest while he escorted her outside the ring. What had gotten into her? She wasn't the type to be affectionate in public with anyone. Her ex-boyfriend even mentioned it several times, but here she stood making out with a guy she barely knew in a bar in his hometown. *Good gravy.* She'd turned into a regular slut in this small cowboy town.

"Don't be embarrassed."

"I don't do these sort of things, Joel."

"It's okay. Nobody even noticed."

She lifted her face from his chest and caught the dirty looks from the women as well as the thumbs up from several of the men surrounding them.

"Okay. So a few noticed."

"A few? If looks could kill, I'd be dead from the dirty looks the women are giving me, especially Brandy."

"Don't worry about it. Come on. Let's dance." He led her out onto the dance floor, put her hand on his shoulder, and took her other hand in his. "Now, relax. The step is called a two-step. You step once, shuffle twice and step again."

She took a deep breath, trying to concentrate on his words as he slowly led her around the dance floor.

"You're doin' great." He touched a finger under her chin to make her lift her gaze to his. "See? It's not so hard."

She stepped on his toe. "God, I'm sorry."

"It's okay. It's happened before. You aren't the first lady to step on my toes."

"I'm not supposed to, though. You're such a patient teacher." His gaze pulled her in as the music faded out of her conscious thought. She'd never seen eyes the color of his. Blue like a glacier, or maybe a swimming pool. She could so drown in his stare. The five o'clock shadow of a beard on his face made him sexier. Rugged. So fucking hot.

The music changed to something slow. A song she recognized. Dustin Lynch's *Cowboys and Angels*. *Damn. This is my favorite song.* Why does Joel have to be so gorgeous? Why can't he be some scraggly old codger who would be willing to tell her all his cowboy secrets over a cup of coffee? *And holy hell, there are three of him! Fuckin' A.*

"You slow dance well," he whispered, nuzzling her ear.

"There isn't much to it, really. You just shuffle back and forth. I probably won't bruise your toes on this one."

"We could always try a faster song. I can swing dance, too." He laughed at the shocked look on her face.

"Oh, hell no. I got your feet with the simple two-step. I'd probably break something swing dancing."

"I like this better anyway. I can hold you closer."

"You were holding me pretty close with the two-step."

"Not close enough." He pulled her in tighter. Her breasts brushed against the front of his western shirt, making them peak like mountaintops reaching for the warmth of the sky. *Damn, traitorous nipples.* "Are you excited, Mesa?"

"Excited?"

"Are your panties wet?" he whispered, brushing those full lips over her ear.

"A bit bold, aren't you?"

"I know when a woman is excited."

"Not this woman."

"Really?" he asked with a raised eyebrow over those damn sexy eyes. "Your nipples are poking me in the chest. Cold?"

"Why yes, I am."

"Liar." His lips brush her neck.

Her eyes drifted closed as goose bumps danced down her arms. His hands settled on her hips, slowly dragging her into the warmth of his embrace. *God, the man was sex on a stick.* Did he think she was some loser in the bedroom that he could drag into his web with eyes blue enough to drown in, lips full enough to lose her mind, and a body to stop traffic at a green light?

Of course he did.

She stepped out of his embrace. "I need a drink." She blew the hair off her forehead with a frustrated breath.

"I thought you were cold?" he asked with a smirk.

"Smartass."

"But yours is cute enough to eat whipped cream off of."

Fuck! She was so screwed. *If he wants to get me into the sack, he's doing a damn good job of it, even if I want it too.* "I thought you weren't supposed to seduce the guests?"

"Seduce? Who me?" He grinned as he wrapped his arm around her waist to escort her to the bar. "Beer?"

"Sure."

"Two Buds in the bottle please," he said, signaling the bartender who responded with a nod.

"Someone you know?"

"I know everyone in here, pretty much. We also know the judge, the sheriff, the lawyers, the schoolteachers, the principal, and everyone else. Most all of those you see in here now are guys and gals I went to high school with." He reached up to wave to someone nearby.

"I don't know what it's like to be surrounded by people I've grown up with."

"No?"

"Nope. I went to a high school where my graduating class had three thousand kids in it."

"Holy shit! Mine had one hundred fifty and I thought it was huge. It took three hours to read all the names off."

He paid the bartender before he handed her the bottle, then tipped his to his sensuous lips. *Lordy, the man could kiss.* The slow glide of his mouth over hers earlier in the dark, had been enough to curl her toes, but the lip smacking, tongue tangling kiss he'd laid on her after her bull ride still had her panting for air. She tentatively sipped at her beer, hoping it would wash away the taste of the kiss. No luck. She could still feel his mouth on hers. The slide of his tongue. *Damn.*

"Mine had to be split into two days. A through L one day and M through Z the next day. It sucks living in such a large place sometimes. I like having things to do all the time like shopping and stuff, but it's crazy not knowing who your neighbors are."

"I don't think I could live somewhere like that. I'm so used to living here. I couldn't be comfortable in a place where I didn't know the guy living above me. Concrete jungle comes to mind."

"Yeah. Now that you mention it, I don't care for it much either."

"Why do you stay then?"

"Because it's home. My parents are there. My siblings are nearby. I've lived in the same neighborhood for five years. I know where everything is."

He wrapped his arm around her waist to tuck her in close to his side. "Haven't you ever wanted to move to a place you didn't know anyone? Learn a new town, a new city?"

"You're one to talk, Joel. You've lived in Bandera all your life."

"True and I love it here. I love the area. I love my neighbors. I love working the ranch with my brothers and I hope someday the woman I marry with learn to love it like I do."

"Tall order."

"Not really."

"I guess not if you plan to marry someone who is already from here. They'd fit right in." He bent down and kissed her. "What was that for?" she asked, bewildered by his behavior.

"Just to let you know I'm thinking of you right at the moment. Not someone else."

"Thanks...I think." She wrinkled her nose. He laughed.

"It's a compliment, Mesa. You're a beautiful woman. I'm glad I'm here with you."

"You confuse me, Joel."

"Why?"

"Because one minute you kiss me and tell me I'm beautiful. The next I'm not sure if you're talking about me or someone else you've been with recently."

His mouth pulled down at the corners when he frowned. "What gave you the idea I was talking about anyone but you?"

"Just...oh never mind."

"I'm with you tonight. I think it's rude to talk about other women when you're with one."

She shrugged. "But we aren't together. We're here as friends."

"Still."

"Let's just have a good time. Forget about the rest for now."

"Sounds good to me. Are you finished with your beer? I want to dance with you again."

"And have me stepping on your feet more?"

"You're so cute when you're joking," he said, tweaking her nose, and then brushing his mouth against hers.

What the hell was she going to do about these feelings? She wanted to jump him and ride his hips into tomorrow like some rodeo bronc rider, but on the other hand, getting involved with a guy like him in a situation like this was a sure way to feel like shit when she went back to L.A.

He swept her up in his arms the minute they hit the dance floor again, doing a quick two-step. The dance brought her close enough to smell him. She wanted to taste him. Find out if his skin tasted salty under her tongue. Did he have a little sweat she could lick off?

"What are you thinking about?'

'Nothin', why?"

"You've got a guilty little smirk on your lips."

She captured her lips between her teeth.

"Ah, somethin' dirty?"

"Maybe, but I won't tell."

"How about if I tickle you until you tell me?"

"You wouldn't." His hand curled into her side and she giggled like a schoolgirl. "That's not fair!"

"Sure it is. You're keeping secrets."

"I'm a woman. We have secrets."

"Tell me." He tickled her again.

"Stop!"

"Not until you tell me."

"Okay, okay!" She gasped for breath as he led them to an empty table toward the back of the bar in a secluded corner. How this particular table became available, she would never know, but here she sat with one the most gorgeous men she'd ever seen in a darkened corner.

"Spill it."

"I was thinking about you."

"Me?"

"Yeah."

"And?"

She forced a ragged breath between her lips. Surely he didn't really expect her to tell him she wanted to lick the sweat from his body after he fucked her like a couple of bunny rabbits? "Nothing, really." He reached over and tickled her side. "All right!" She sighed. "You are rotten, you know?"

He touched her side again, making her jump.

"I was thinking about you being sweaty."

"Like after working outside?"

"Yeah."

"Why would you be thinking about me being sweaty?"

"Like licking you after sex." Heat crawled up her neck as she dropped her gaze to the table. "I'm so embarrassed."

"Why?"

"Seriously? We've only known each other like not even twenty-four hours."

"So? I think you're beautiful, sexy, interesting, and a great dancer. There's nothing wrong with being attracted to each other." He reached over and slid his hand along the side of her face. "I want to kiss you."

"You've kissed me before," she whispered, drowning in his eyes.

"I want to do it again."

His breath flittered across her lips. She wanted his mouth. She wanted his tongue. God, she wanted all of him touching her, holding her, making love to her.

"We should go."

"No. Not until I've tasted you again."

"Hey, Joel. Mesa," Josh said, sliding into the booth on the other side of her.

"Josh. What are you doing here?"

"I saw your two leave and figured you might be headed here."

Shit. Now I'm sandwiched between two good-looking men. Threesome? No, no, no.

"Yeah, we did. We've been dancing."

"I rode the bull," she said, moving a little further away from Joel. She needed the breathing room. Being close to him did all kinds of funny things to her insides.

"You did? Wow. Great job!" Josh exclaimed. "Did Joel?"

"No."

"Chicken, brother?"

"No. I got busy congratulating Mesa and forgot."

"Uh-huh."

The look on Joshua's didn't face bode well for their continued anonymity. She really didn't want his family knowing about their shared kisses or the fact of her wanting to get him in bed. She needed to forget about that part. He really should be beyond her reach. Girls like her didn't get guys like him. Women like Brandy roped in guys like the triplets, with their penetrating blue gazes, rock hard bodies, and kissable, full lips. *Damn.*

"Dance with me, Mesa," Joshua said, holding out his hand. "Please?"

"I'll warn you, I step on toes."

"No, she doesn't," Joel added. "She just learned to two-step though, so take it easy on her."

"Of course, brother."

She scooted out of the booth, allowing Joshua to take her hand and lead her to the dance floor. The whole time, she felt Joel's gaze on her back. The moment they reached the wood flooring, Joshua swept her up in his arms, bringing her in close…too close. She pushed on his chest to put more space between them. "Ease up on the hold buddy, or you're gonna lose something precious to you."

"Come on. You like Joel. I can see it in your eyes. We're identical."

"In looks maybe. But you need to think about what you're doing here." She pushed again.

"What? I'm dancing with a pretty woman."

"Who happens to be here with your brother."

"So?"

"You don't get it, do you? Do you guys always fight over women?"

'No." He grinned and winked. "I usually win."

"Why? Because you're an ass if you ask me."

He put one hand on his chest. "I'm hurt, Mesa. I thought you were a nice girl."

"I am, but I don't put up with bullshit like what you're trying to pull. Let me go."

"I could make it good for you. Joel won't go against the wishes of our mother and I think you want a good, hard lay."

She pushed out of his arms, pulled back her arm and slapped him as hard as she could. "How dare you! Someday you're going to find a woman who will put you in your place, Josh, and I'm going to laugh my ass off when I see it. Joel is twice the man you are."

"What's going on?" Joel asked, sliding to a stop between her and Josh.

"Nothing. Josh was just leaving."

"No I'm not."

"Yeah, you are brother. You've obviously insulted my lady friend and I won't put up with it. Go home before I kick your ass."

"You can try."

"Take it outside boys," the bartender hollered from behind the bar. "No fighting in here. You know the rules."

"Fine. Outside?" Josh asked, egging on his brother by smiling at Mesa.

"Bring it on, bro. I can kick your ass anytime."

"Stop this!" she shouted, pulling on Joel's arm. "Don't do this. Don't fight over nothing."

"It's not nothin', darlin'. He insulted you or you wouldn't have slapped him."

Joel followed Josh to the door with Mesa following close on their heels. A crowd of people trailed behind her. Surely it wasn't anything unusual for the Young brothers to fight? With nine of them, it couldn't be that big of a deal, right?

"Joel, please."

"No, Mesa. He's been asking for this since he came onto you at the barn this afternoon. He thinks he can do whatever he pleases and there aren't any consequences. Well there will be tonight."

The moment they cleared the parking lot, Joshua spun around to rush Joel, pushing him up against the side of someone's pickup.

"Fucker!"

"Kiss my ass, brother, and leave my girl alone."

"She ain't your girl, dumbass. You've known her what, six hours?"

Joel pushed Joshua back and swung, connecting with his jaw. Mesa flinched at the bone jarring sound, not sure if it was Joel's knuckles or Joshua's jaw. Josh took a swing, splitting Joel's lip. Blood spurted everywhere.

"You'll pay for that." Joel jabbed Josh in the ribs, doubling him over as he grunted in pain. "I told you I could take you down, asshole. Just go home."

"I'm gonna kick your ass," Joshua wheezed, rolling over onto his side.

"You can't even get up, Josh. Just stay down."

"Fucker!"

"It's not worth it. Go home."

"I'll go when I'm damned good and ready!" Josh rolled to his stomach and pulled his knees under him as he attempted to stand. One hand braced his ribs. "You fuckin' broke my ribs!"

"You asked for it by being a jerk to Mesa."

"She's just a piece of ass, Joel."

Joel swung again, connecting with Joshua's jaw. The blow took Josh flat on his back and out cold.

"He's unconscious!"

"Good. At least he won't get up again."

"You can't leave him like this." Mesa dropped down on the ground near Joshua's head. Josh moaned but didn't open his eyes.

"The hell I can't!"

"At least call one of your other brothers to come, Joel. He's your brother."

"He deserved it." Joel wiped at the blood on his lip with the back of his hand, smearing it across his chin.

"I know he did, but please?"

"Fine." Joe grabbed his brother's arm and hoisted him over his shoulder. "He's ridin' in the back."

"All right."

"Get in. I guess our night is over." He sounded disappointed.

Within moments, they were speeding down the road back toward the ranch with Joshua in the bed of the truck. He'd regained consciousness from what she could tell by looking out the window, but he didn't sit up or anything, just stared at the stars.

"He'll be fine. Mom will take care of him when we get home."

"I'm sorry," she murmured, feeling like shit for causing Joel and Joshua to fight. Of course, she'd never had two men fight over her before, much less two who looked like they did.

"For what?" He glanced her way, then out the windshield of his truck.

"For causing you two to fight."

"He asked for it, Mesa. Besides, it's not like it's the first time we've fought. We've done it for years off and on. It's what brothers do." He banged his hand on the steering wheel. "You didn't do anythin'. He treated you like shit and I won't have it. He can be a nice guy when he's not drinking, but get a little alcohol in him and he turns into a jerk." He glanced her way again. "Why are you being so nice to him? He called you a piece of ass."

"I'm not going to let it bother me, Joel. He's a guy. It's what guys do. Since I know it's not true, it doesn't matter to me."

"But what about all the people at the bar? They probably think we're having sex."

"What do I care? I'll probably never see them again. You and I know we aren't." She placed her hand on his thigh. "They are people. Nothing more."

"You're a better person than I am then. I don't like worrying about what other people think but it's in my nature, I guess. I've always had to fight to be an individual since I'm a triplet. It's hard to make people realize you are who you are rather than just one of the Young boys and a troublemaker."

"I suppose you got into trouble a lot as a kid?"

"Sometimes. I'm the middle of us triplets so it was pretty rough."

"I'm sorry."

"Nothin' to be sorry for. It's how it was."

They pulled up to the gate of the ranch, the headlights reflecting off the wrought iron fence. Joel punched in the code and the bulky piece of metal slowly slid open.

"Where are we?" Josh asked from the back while they bumped along the road toward the house.

Joel slid the window on the back open. "Home, you jackass," Joel called from inside the cab. "You'd better apologize to Mesa. What you said was totally inappropriate."

"Sorry, Mesa."

"I accept your apology. You know, if you act this juvenile when you drink, maybe you shouldn't drink."

"Wait a damned minute. I don't act like a kid."

She raised an eyebrow and smirked. "Are you sure?"

"All right maybe a little, but it's only in fun."

"It's not fun when someone's feelings get hurt."

"Did I hurt your feelings, Mesa?"

"It's not important."

"Yes, it is. If Mom found out you acted like an idiot, she'd tan your hide," Joel answered even though the question wasn't directed toward him.

"I'm too old for a whuppin'."

"Not from Mom. You know how she is about disrespecting women." Joel stopped the truck before he went around to open her door.

"Thank you."

"For what?"

"Opening my door."

"Sorry. I don't think about it. It's been ingrained in us since we were old enough to know manners."

"It's still a nice gesture and I appreciate it."

"You're welcome."

"I'm headed to my place. If Mom sees me, she really will tan my hide." Josh touched his chin. "Damn, dude! Did you have to hit me so fuckin' hard?"

"Don't think I'm not tellin' her what you did and yes I did. You were an ass."

"I already apologized, Joel. Let it go."

She placed her hand on Joel's arm to get his attention. "It's fine. He did apologize."

Joshua kissed her cheek before he headed off toward what she assumed to be his house. She could see a small, cabin like structure outlined in the distance. She'd have to check it out in the daylight although she didn't want to encourage Joshua, only Joel. "Let me clean up the cut on your lip."

He touched it and winced. "You don't have to. It'll be okay."

"You were gallant in standing up for me the way you did. It's the least I could do." They walked toward the main lodge in companionable silence. She really wasn't sure what to think with Joel. He acted like he was attracted to her, but then he wouldn't go against the rules of the ranch it seemed. They could be friends only, she supposed, although she wanted him hot between the sheets.

As they walked in the side doorway, she caught a glimpse of a cowboy walking out through the front door and wondered who he was. She thought she'd met all of those working the ranch during dinner. "Do you have someone not in the family working as a wrangler at the ranch?"

"No. Why?"

"I thought I saw someone I didn't recognize walk outside."

Joel shrugged. "It was probably one of my brothers."

"Maybe. He looked older."

"My dad?"

"Could have been I guess."

"Let me grab your key from the office. Your room is upstairs."

"Sure," she answered although he'd already walked away. A chill raced down her back and she rubbed her arms. *Weird.* It's still like seventy degrees outside even though her watch read eleven when she glanced at the dial.

Joel came back with a grin on his face but frowned the moment his lip started to bleed again. "Damn Josh. My lip hurts."

"Poor baby. You'll be fine. He got the worst part of the deal, I think." She grabbed his hand and said, "Lead the way."

They walked toward the wooden staircase at the back of the room hand in hand, but she stopped to look behind her for a moment.

"Something wrong?"

"I thought…" She shook her head and started walking again. "Never mind."

He led her up the first flight of stairs to the door in front of them and handed her the old fashioned key on a tag. "Wow. I haven't seen one of these in a long time. I didn't think anyone used these anymore."

"We do. We don't have the fancy credit card sliders like most other hotels and motels. This is a small, family run dude ranch."

"I wasn't critizing, Joel. I think it's cool you guys are regular country people." She slipped the key into the lock and opened the door. Mesa walked over to turn on the lamp on the bedside table, bathing the room in soft, muted light. Dominating the smaller room stood a double bed with a beautiful wedding ring comforter. Her clean clothes sat in a nice neat pile by the pillows. A wooden dresser sat at the end of the bed and to the right. The single large window overlooked the garden behind the house. Something she would have to explore tomorrow. She loved gardens. Right now, it looked spooky bathed in moonlight but romantic at the same time.

"The garden is my mother's favorite place to hang out. She's got lots of flowers back there, a sitting bench, a swing, and a barbeque. We throw parties out there during the cooler months."

"Texas does get warm in the summer."

"It's been pretty here this week. Not too hot and not too cold."

"Just for me."

He laughed. "Maybe."

"Except for the rain shower today."

"Those are normal for this time of year too."

"Just my luck."

"If you give me the keys to your car, I'll grab your suitcase and bring it up."

"All right." She handed him the keys. "On one condition. You let me wash the cut on your lip."

"Yes, nurse."

She startled a little, and then smiled.

"What?"

"I always wanted to be a nurse."

"Then why didn't you?" He held up his hand. "Wait to answer that until I get back." A moment later, he closed the door behind him, disappearing from sight.

Mute voices drifted through the wall. *Must be some other guests in the room next door.* The man's voice rose in anger. She cringed knowing where those tones usually led. She heard a slap, and then muffled crying a moment later. The sound died away after a few seconds as if it had never been there in the first place.

Mesa frowned, rubbing her arms as the room dropped in temperature like the air conditioner kicked on, but it hadn't. She shook her head and went to the connecting bathroom to fetch a warm washcloth to clean Joel's lip. The bathroom was decorated in the typical old-fashioned way with wood accents. A claw foot tub with a shower curtain to one end, and a large showerhead reminded her of the rain showerhead she had at home. Maybe tomorrow night she would take a long soak in the huge tub. A soft knock on the door brought her out of her musings.

She quickly grabbed a washcloth from those hanging on the rack, stuck it under some hot water and went to answer the door. She opened it to find no one on the other side. After she leaned out, she glanced down the hallway to both the left and right without seeing anyone nearby. "All right, Joel. That's not funny. You're scaring me."

"What are you talking about, Mesa?" he asked, coming up the stairs in front of her. "Who are you talking to?"

"Uh. No one, I guess."

"I've got your suitcase."

She stepped aside to allow him into the room. "Just set it on the bed and I'll unpack it in a minute." She told him to sit on the edge of the bed as she took a spot between his spread thighs. She exhaled forcibly through her lips so she could focus on the task at hand and not his hard thighs now encasing her lower half. The cut on his lip didn't look too deep. With her finger inside the cloth, she dabbed at the cut.

"Ouch."

"Sorry."

"It's okay. I know you didn't mean to hurt me."

He winced as she dabbed again. It had to hurt, she knew but all she could think about was kissing those full lips. She wanted to see his eyes dark with desire. Feel his hands on her bare flesh. Have those lips on other places of her body like her breasts, her nipples, or her clit.

"You okay?" he whispered, glancing up through those impossibly long eyelashes.

"Yeah." Her heart pounded behind her ribcage.

"Your pulse is fluttering."

"I know."

"Why?" His voice continued in a soft, coaxing tone reminding her of how he spoke to the horse while she gave birth to her foal.

"It's nothing, Joel."

"Do you want me to kiss you?"

She closed her eyes and licked her lips. *God, do I ever want you to kiss me. More than my next breath. More than a winning lottery ticket. More than...*

The next thing she knew, he had twisted her around so she lay flat on the bed with him hovering over her. He bent down and brushed his lips against hers so softly she wasn't sure if he'd actually kissed her.

"You shouldn't be doing this."

"I know."

He kissed her again, this time with his tongue softly brushing her lips as if to ask for permission to deepen it. Her lips parted of their own accord without her even thinking beyond how his lips felt against hers. The dip of his tongue tore a moan from her mouth. She tangled her hands in the front of his western shirt, wanting nothing more than to remove the barrier between his skin and hers.

The fire burning in her gut prompted her to return kiss for kiss, touch for touch. The caress of his fingers against the side of her breast brought her straight up on the bed, breaking the kiss.

"What's wrong?"

"I...uh. We shouldn't do this. Remember your mother's rule."

"I know, but I can't help but want to touch you. Kiss you." He ran his fingers down her cheek. "You're a beautiful woman, Mesa. I'm not sorry."

She touched her fingers to her lips as he turned to go.

"Goodnight, Mesa."

"Goodnight, Joel."

Chapter Six

"Stupid, Joel. Really, really stupid!" He threw the horse's bridle across the tack room before he raked his fingers through his hair, knocking his Stetson from his head.

"Whoa. What's got your panties in a twist?" Jacob asked, putting one of the saddles back on the rack. "You aren't usually this strung up."

"Nothin'."

"It doesn't sound like nothin' to me. Throwing tack usually means you're pissed."

"Fine. I'm pissed."

Jacob removed his hat and tossed it on the desk in the corner. "About?"

"A woman."

"So?"

"It's Mesa." He paced from one side of the tack room to the other with agitated steps. The thing with Mesa had him wound up tighter than a string of barbwire.

"Ah."

"I kissed her."

"Yeah, we all saw it out by the bonfire."

"No, after that. More than once."

"I still don't understand what the big deal is."

"I can't get involved with someone who is only going to be here for a few days. It's crazy."

"So you have a quick fling. What's the problem?"

He stopped and turned to face his brother. "The big deal is she's not the kind of girl you have a quick fling with, Jacob. She's a nice girl. The kind of girl you settle down with."

"Seriously, Joel. Settle down?"

"I'm not thinkin' of settlin' down, idiot, but she's not the barfly type."

"Maybe she is. You never know." He picked up the bridle and hung it on the rack. "Maybe you should ask her?"

"Ask her? Really? What do I say? How about a quick fuck, Mesa?"

"Sure. Why not?"

Joel picked up his Stetson and put it back on his head. "Maybe. I mean she's attracted to me from what I can tell. She definitely got into the kiss we shared."

"Just fuck her already, would ya," Jason added, coming in from the corral. "I'll take her off your hands if you want. Not like she could tell the difference between us anyway."

"I bet she could."

"I bet she couldn't."

Joel stuck out his hand. "How much?"

"A hundred bucks," Jason answered.

"You're on."

"Fine. After dinner, I'll take her up to her room and turn on the charm. I bet she kisses me and lets me feel her up."

Joel squinted and snapped, "I bet she calls a halt to everything after the first kiss if not before."

"You know very few people outside of the family can tell the difference between us, Joel. I bet she can't."

"I think she's more into me and will be able to tell right away." Joel kicked a rock near the toe of his boot back out into the corral. He sounded confident to his brother, but he wasn't so sure. What if Mesa couldn't tell the difference? What if she liked Jason better than him? *No, this is nuts. I know what our kiss was like. We could set the sheets on fire if I could get her between them.* "I know what I felt when we kissed."

"She's just a woman, Joel. Nothin' special."

"You're wrong there, Jason. She is special."

* * * *

The dinner bell clanged and Mesa frowned. She hadn't seen Joel all day. Was he avoiding her? Probably. Men didn't take well to being put off when they had sex on the brain. Stopping their kiss the night before wasn't a bad idea, but maybe he felt like there wasn't anything to gain now by hanging out with her.

As Mesa made her way down the stairs to the dining room, the sound of voices got louder. A bus full of tourist had arrived earlier in the day, making the whole place buzz like a swarm of bees. Many of them went riding earlier, leaving her the run of the ranch house to herself. She'd taken her laptop into the main hall, set it up on one of the tables and managed to type out the beginning of a new novel called Mission: Cowboy. She cringed. She wasn't sure she liked it, but she figured a new title would come to her when the characters started adding their voices to the storyline. She wasn't a plotter when it came to her stories so everything depended on what they said.

Stopping on the stairs, she looked over the group. All the tourists were back and the place was packed to the gills. The family waited at their table for the group to be served while they chatted about their day. Joel sat at the end of the table next to an empty chair she hoped might be for her. Or was it Joshua? Maybe Jason? *Damn.* From this distance she wasn't sure which one was which? *Damn it.*

"Mesa, come sit by me, darlin'." One of the three waved from the end of the table.

She chewed on her lips a moment and then started down the stairs. *Okay. Joel? Shit. I'm not sure.* She took the seat he held out for her, dropping into it with little grace. *Nice, Mesa.*

"How was your day?"

"Great. I got a lot of writing done in the main lodge."

"Awesome."

The rest of the group had been served, so the family got up to get their own plates, which included her. Joel or whichever one of them this was standing next to her, grinned and motioned for her to take the spot in front of him. His cologne drifted to her nose. It seemed different somehow. She looked closer. No, she couldn't really tell if it was Joel, Jason, or Joshua. Well, yes she could because Joshua had a small cut near his chin and Joel had a small abrasion near his bottom lip from their fight at the bar last night. This must be Jason. But what was he up to? Was he deliberately playing like she didn't know the difference? Surely they didn't think she was that stupid.

"I enjoyed our kiss last night," he whispered near her ear.

Okay, she didn't like this game. What the hell was going on? "Really? I'm glad."

"Me too. I want to take you out in the moonlight tonight after dinner. You game?"

"Okay." She frowned. *Really?* She grabbed a plate in order to get her dinner as the conversation lagged. Discussing this in front of his family wasn't a great idea. She glanced around looking for Joel. He stood at the back of the line frowning. What kind of game were they playing?

She returned to her place at the table, setting her plate down first before she retrieved a glass of lemonade and a dessert. Jason slid his hand along her shoulder as he took the seat next to her. Now she knew why the cologne was different, he wasn't Joel. Why was Joel giving her the cold shoulder? What did they plan?

The conversation around the table focused on the day's labors. They'd moved cattle from the south pasture to the north pasture. Several of the cattle had dropped their calves already making everyone worry it might be too late in the season and they would suffer without extra feed. She could hear many of the tourists talking about their ride on the horses that day and she mentally planned to do some riding of her own tomorrow. Horseback riding was one of her favorite past times. She wanted to explore the ranch more with Joel, though. Not on a strict trail ride.

"Would you like to go riding tomorrow?" Jason asked.

"Um, yes I would."

"Great. I'll saddle a couple of horses. I can meet you at the stable around nine in the morning."

"Okay." *What the hell? This whole thing stinks.*

They finished dinner in silence while the rest of the family talked about different topics. The moment she finished, Jason grabbed her plate to deposit it into the dirty dish bin.

"Walk with me."

"All right," she answered, deciding to see where this whole thing might be leading. Did Joel push her off on his brother because he didn't want to hurt her feelings by saying he wasn't attracted to her? Did Jason think she wanted him?

She let Jason take her hand and walk her out the front door of the main lodge to the chairs lining the porch. Even though the full moon happened the night before, it still shone bright enough to see the walkway.

"You look beautiful in the moonlight."

"Thank you."

"You know, the kiss we shared last night blew my socks off. I wish you hadn't made me leave."

Frowning, she opened her mouth to tell him she knew he wasn't Joel, but he bent his head and kissed her full on the mouth. She quickly stepped back and smacked him across the face. "How dare you."

"What?"

"Do you think I'm stupid? Do both of you think I wouldn't know the difference between you, Jason?"

"You knew I wasn't Joel?"

"Hell yes! Even if I hadn't figured it out at dinner, I would have known from the kiss."

"Most people can't tell the difference between us."

"Joel has an abrasion near the left side of his mouth from where he got in a fight with Joshua at the bar last night."

"Damn."

"What the hell is going on here? Why the ruse?"

"I'll tell you, Mesa," Joel said, coming around the side of the house. "I was pissed off at myself this morning because of what happened last night. Our kiss, I mean."

"Well you know what? Fuck both of you! You want to play these sillyassed games, you can play them on some other unsuspecting woman. I'm not doin' it."

"Mesa, listen," Joel implored, holding out his hand to touch her arm.

She jerked back and slapped at him. "No. This is childish. I can't believe you two! I thought I might have meant a little more to you than this, Joel, but apparently not. What we shared last night was special to me, but not to you. I'm just another girl to you."

"No, you're not, Mesa."

"Yeah, whatever." She spun around to head back into the house. Maybe it was time to go. Head back to Los Angeles and lick her wounds.

"Mesa, please."

"What Joel?" She turned back around.

"Let's talk about this."

"What the hell is there to talk about? You and your brother were playing me for the fool. How many times have you three switched places on a girl, huh? I bet a lot."

"No."

"Yes." During her discussion with Joel, Jason had disappeared either back into the house or whatever. At this point, she really didn't care. He probably slinked back into his hidy hole. Man, if she ever became a permanent part of this family, she'd…what? *Those are crazy thoughts.*

Joel slipped his hand along the side of her face before burying his hand in her hair. He dragged her in closer with a fistful of her hair at the back of her neck. "I want you."

"You made a fool of me."

"No, I wanted to make sure it was me you wanted." His lips whispered over hers. The softness skimmed across her cheek to her ear. "I need you."

"Need is a powerful word."

"It's totally what I'm feeling, but I can't promise you anything beyond tonight."

"I don't need anything more."

"Are you sure?" he asked, listing his head to look into her eyes. The blue glistened in the moonlight like a beacon for her lost soul.

"Yes. I need you. I need this."

"Your room or my place?"

"You have somewhere we can go?"

"Yeah. I have my own cabin a few miles up the road."

"Make love to me, Joel. Fuck me."

He pulled her head back as he raked his teeth along her neck. Shivers raced down her arms as a soft moan escaped her mouth. "Come home with me."

"Yes, please."

He looked deep into her eyes for a moment as if judging whether she was serious or not. Little did he know, she'd wanted this from the first time he'd kissed her or maybe it was when she had her breasts squished to his back as they rode in the rain back to the house? Who cared?

"Let's go," he said, grabbing her hand and half dragging her to where his truck stood in the parking lot behind the main lodge.

"A little horny are we?"

"Hell yeah. A lot horny. You've had me wound up tighter than a damned spring from the moment you climbed up behind me to rest those gorgeous breasts against my back." He opened the door on the driver's side of his truck, practically shoving her inside the cab by the seat of her pants. "Sorry, baby."

Oh I love the little endearments coming from his mouth now that we're going to have sex. "You can call me all the little pet names you want."

He grinned as he turned over the truck and shot gravel behind it as he tore out of the drive. "You have no idea how much I want this."

"If I'm judging your craving to mine, I bet I do."

"How long has it been since you've had sex?"

"Several months. You?"

"Me too."

"You do have condoms, right?"

"Yeah. A few." He grinned.

"I hope you plan on using several tonight."

"Oh, no problem there, babe."

Damn, he almost sounds cocky. Well, why wouldn't he be? He could probably have any woman he wants. She frowned, feeling a bit self-conscious at her rounded little stomach and even rounder hips. She wasn't a skinny woman by any means.

"Why the frown?"

"Nothing."

"No, baby. Tell me. No secrets tonight."

She bit her lip.

"Come on."

"I'm just not the skinny little cowgirls you're used to."

"I'm not into skinny."

"Younger?"

"I'm not into jailbait either, Mesa. I like you the way you are. Rounded curves and enough softness for me to sink myself into. I don't plan on coming out until tomorrow mornin'. You okay with that?"

"Are you sure?"

"Positive, babe." He grabbed her hand to place it on his groin.

The hardness behind his fly let her know he wanted her…needed her. *God, he's huge!*

"I hope you plan on goin' easy on me."

"Why?"

"Like I said, I haven't had sex in a bit and you aren't exactly small."

"I'll take care of you."

Within moments, they pulled up to a small cabin with a porch around the front. It wasn't anything huge by any means. Just small enough for a single man, or a couple maybe. *Get those thoughts out of your head. You're only here for a few days.*

"Nice place."

"Thanks. It's not much, but it's got a king sized bed."

"That'll do for tonight then." *King sized bed and Joel for the night? Hell yeah!*

No lights shone from the windows. White curtains blew in the breeze of the one open to the left front corner. The house wasn't decorated at all. No woman's touch anywhere.

"Sorry. It's kind of a mess."

"A bachelor lives here. I wouldn't expect anything else." Dishes were piled in the small sink to her right as they walked through the door. He had a stove, refrigerator and a few cabinets to hold dishes, she assumed. The couch in front of the fireplace would make for great cozy nights. She shook her head. She didn't need to go there.

"This way." He took her hand and led her back down the hall to the first door on the right. "There's a bathroom to your left if you need it."

"Thanks," she said, walking through the small doorway and shutting it behind her. The florescent lighting over the mirror showed her wild hair from Joel running his hands through it. Her eyes were bright. The pupils dilated. Her lips were puffy from his kiss. All in all, she looked like a slut. "Great." She ran her fingers through her hair to try and straighten it out a little before she went back out there. "Okay, really Mesa. I don't think he cares what your hair looks like except if it's the hair between your legs."

Oh, crap! I didn't shave my legs this morning. What if they are stubbly? I didn't shave my bikini line lately either. Shit!

"Mesa? Are you okay, babe?"

"I'm fine, Joel. I'll be out in a second."

"I've got some wine. We can sit and relax for a bit. No hurry on this." It sounded like he ran his knuckles on the door. "I mean, we can talk a while or whatever."

"Okay." Could he tell her nerves were shot? Probably. He definitely was trying to soothe them. She used the restroom, washed her hands, and then opened the door. Joel stood on the other side with a little smile lifting the corners of his mouth.

"Better?"

"Yeah. Thanks."

"Come with me," he said, taking her hand. With his hat now gone the light reflected in a blue-black sheen on his curls. "We can watch television, talk or whatever you want to do. We don't even have to have sex if you've changed your mind."

"I haven't. Have you?" she asked, taking a seat next to him on the couch.

"No, but I don't want you to think I'm some kind of caveman. You're comfort means everything to me."

She wiped her sweaty palms along the thighs of her jeans.

"Are you nervous?"

"Yeah, a little," she said with a shrug. "I've never had casual sex before."

He ran his fingers along her jaw. "I've never been in a relationship, so I guess it makes us even."

"Never?"

"Well, nothin' serious anyway. I've dated a couple of women for a period of time, but it never got serious on my part."

She frowned. He smoothed his thumb between her eyes.

"What's the frown for?"

"I was thinking about my ex."

"A hint here, Mesa. Guys don't want to hear you're thinking about your ex when they're about to have sex with you."

She turned to face him as she placed her hand on his chest. "No, nothing like that. I wasn't comparing you by any means. There's nothing to compare with. I mean, you're lean, muscular and drop dead gorgeous. Those eyes could melt chocolate and you know how much women love chocolate. He didn't have any of those things."

"What were you comparing then?"

"I wasn't comparing anything. I had a thought about how my relationship with him seems so different than this with you. When I went out with him, things moved very slowly. We didn't have sex for six months after we met. Even then, it wasn't anything to write home about." With a giggle, she covered her mouth. "Not like I would write my mother about my sex life, but you know what I mean."

He laughed. "Yeah, I do. There've been a few women I wouldn't make love to twice."

"Really? I thought all guys were just in it for the end result. You know, gettin' their rocks off."

"Not if they are any good, they aren't. It's more fun for me to make sure the woman has several orgasms when I'm with her."

The lump in her throat almost choked her. "Several?"

He leaned in and ran his tongue along her jawline until he reached her ear. "Yeah, several."

Holy shit, he's got one sexy voice. The lower rumble of his voice threw her heart into overdrive. The slow seep of moisture between her thighs surprised her. She never got this wet with her ex. Not from only a whisper in her ear. Those were things she wrote about in her novels, not something she experienced for herself. She swallowed *hard*.

"Um, Joel?"

"Yeah?" he asked, sliding his tongue around her earlobe.

"Damn, you're good."

He chuckled softly as he nipped the fleshy part of her ear between his teeth. She closed her eyes, letting the feelings overwhelm her. Hooking up with him probably wasn't a good idea, but every time he got close to her, she couldn't think of anything except getting him between the sheets to see how good he really was.

One hand slipped up her stomach to cup her breast. Two of his fingers plucked at her nipple through her bra and her whole world tilted on its axis. She'd always known her nipples were sensitive, but the slight pain of his pinch sent her body into a spiral of need.

His hand disappeared, reappearing under her shirt, pushing her bra out of the way. The warmth of his hand on her breast brought a moan to her lips. Seconds later, her shirt found its way over her head to leave her sitting on his lap in just her bra and jeans.

"God, you're gorgeous. All curves."

"You mean fat."

"No, curves. I love curves on a woman. I'm not into skinny like a rail. I want something to hold onto when I'm pounding my cock into your sweet heat."

"I want you to."

"Shall we head into the other room where it's more comfortable? Not that I wouldn't love to make you come a dozen times right here on the couch first."

"A dozen?" She gulped a lungful of air as shivers raked her body.

"Oh yeah."

He stood with her in his arms and headed down the small hall toward the bedroom. She hadn't got a good look at the bedroom when they came down here before, but she did now. He didn't have a lot of furniture. Just a bed, a small nightstand, and a dresser. The deep blue comforter on the bed seemed typical guy décor. A shade on the window gave him privacy, but did nothing to soften the room. No curtains hung there. Nothing to indicate a woman had ever called this space home. Someday, one would, though. When, she didn't know and didn't want to think about right now, but yeah, someday he would bring a wife here until they could build a bigger home for children.

"You're thinking too much," he whispered, from behind her as he wrapped his arms around her.

"Yeah, probably."

He cupped her breasts in both hands and tugged her back against his chest. "Your skin is so soft. I could eat you up."

"I hope you do."

"Oh, I plan on it, baby. I'm gonna eat you until you scream my name."

"I don't think it'll take much."

"Good." He licked the side of her neck before he nipped at her collarbone. "I can't wait to feel you ripple around me."

He skimmed one hand down her abdomen, flicking open the button at her waist on his way to pulling her zipper down. The moment he had her pants parted, he slipped one hand under the waistband of her underwear to push a finger deep inside her pussy. "You're wet, darlin'."

"You've made me wet, Joel, with your sexy voice, wicked tongue, and demanding nips."

"You'll be wetter before I'm done with you."

"Promises, promises."

"Oh yeah."

She widened her stance to allow him better access as he ran his wet finger over her clit. Her whole body shook. The man was wicked. Sex on a stick.

The elastic of her bra gave way to his insistent fingers, loosening around her breasts until it barely hung on her body. She drew the cups down over her breasts, letting it slide completely off to the floor at her feet. "You need to be undressed, too."

"I will. For now, I'm enjoying your beautiful breasts. I love your nipples. Rosy, hard, and standing straight out. I wish I had a set of nipple clamps for them."

"Nipple clamps?"

"Have you ever had them on?"

"No, but I've heard of them."

"Yours are perfect for a set."

"Thanks."

He pinched her nipples, causing her to close her eyes and moan from deep in her chest. The next thing she felt was his hands on her hips, pushing her pants to the floor. "Step out."

Doing what he told her felt natural, but a little scary. She wasn't one to take orders very well normally. She started to turn around until he held her in place.

"Uh-uh." He pulled her arms behind her, binding her wrist with his hands. "I like my sex a little rough. How about you?"

"What do you mean by rough?"

"Spankings, hard sex. Fuck me like you mean it."

"Spankings? I've never liked those."

"Ever had an erotic spanking?"

"Can't say I have." She shivered as he ran his hands from her breasts to her hips, and then smacked her on the right butt cheek. The groan escaping her mouth surprised her. Maybe she did like erotic spankings after all or spankings in general.

He chuckled as he did it again. "Sounds to me like you enjoy a little pain with your sex."

"Maybe. I've never had anyone do the things you're doing to me before."

"It'll be a brand new experience for you then."

She rubbed her burning butt cheeks against the roughness of his denim jeans. She wondered what it would feel like if he really got going?

"Another time."

Damn the man! Why does it seem like he knows what I'm thinkin'?

"Your eyes are very expressive. I can usually tell what you're thinking by seeing your eyes. Right now, you're turned on by what I did." He pushed his fingers into her pussy. "You can't hide your body's response."

"How can you see my eyes? You're behind me."

"Look toward the dresser."

She hadn't noticed it before but a large mirror reflected their bodies in the most erotic way she'd ever seen. She frowned as she saw the pooch of her stomach and the roundness of her hips.

His handed landed a blow to her thigh. "Ouch."

"That wasn't meant to turn you on. Punishment comes in different forms. You won't frown at this body when you look in the mirror. It's mine for now and I love how it looks."

"But…"

He smacked her thigh again. "Mine. Do you hear me?"

"Yes."

"Now look at it as I see it. Beautiful, high breasts." He cupped her breasts, lifting them. "Gorgeous rosy nipples." He pinched her nipples between his thumb and first finger. "Mine."

"Yours."

His hands skimmed down her abdomen before resting on her hips. "These hips are curvy with just the right amount of padding. I won't have to worry about breaking something if I fuck you hard from behind."

She tried to see herself from his point of view. Her breasts were pretty, still pert with dusky, pink nipples. Her hips were rounded, but those were supposed to be good for child birthing. Long legs. She'd heard men liked long legs. She wasn't fat, really but maybe a little plump.

"You're a beautiful woman, Mesa."

He stood behind her. A head taller than her five foot eight inches making him over six feet. His dark hair curled slightly at the end resting near the nape of his neck. Glacier blue eyes stared back at her in the mirror, dilated widely, and burning hot with lust. They reminded her of a blue flame. The calluses on his hands abrading her skin felt luscious on her body. His five o'clock shadow scraped her shoulders as he rubbed his chin along the slope.

"Cold?" he whispered, running his tongue down her neck.

"No. Excited would be a better word."

"Good. I want you excited." He stepped around her and took her hand, drawing her closer to the big bed in the corner.

With a little tug, he sat her on the edge. Now, he stood directly in front of her, his belt buckle even with her face. Should she touch him? Help him undress? She wasn't sure of the next move.

"Only do as I tell you. I'll make sure you know exactly what to do."

"Okay."

"Unbuckle my belt."

She reached for the large buckle at his waist, slipping the belt through the loops until it had been pulled complete free of his pants. The leather was soft and worn under her touch. *What would it feel like to have him use it on my ass?* She bit her lips in concentration. Should she undo his jeans?

"Some other time we'll play with the belt. I don't want to overload you." He ran the tip of his finger over her bottom lip. "Open my pants."

A soft sigh escaped her lips as he stuck his thumb between her teeth, forcing her mouth open slightly.

"You're gonna suck me. I want to feel those plump lips wrapped around my cock."

Once she got his pants open, she tugged the jeans and his boxers down around his hips so his cock sprang free.

"I don't think I can take all of you."

"You'll do fine, darlin'. I believe in you."

"Can we turn off the lights?"

"No. I want to see you goin' down on me. There's nothin' sexier than a woman's mouth wrapped around my cock."

The heat rising from her chest to splash across her cheeks burned her skin. She wasn't used to being so open with a bed partner. Hell, sex with her ex consisted of lights off and strictly missionary. This was totally different. Sexy. Spontaneous. Hot.

"Take me in your hand. Cup my balls with the other one."

She wrapped her hand around the base of his cock and cupped her hand around the slightly furred sacks below. "Like this?"

"Have you ever given a blow job before, Mesa?"

"Yes, but I want to do this right."

"Do what you want. I'll guide you. You'll be able to tell what feels good for me by the sounds."

She took just the head of his cock between her lips. His hips surged toward her, shoving it a little farther inside her mouth.

"Oh yeah. That's good."

Giving into the notion he enjoyed what she did, she sucked lightly on the head, bringing him more into her mouth. She gagged slightly as he pushed past her palate and hit the back of her throat.

"Breathe through your nose. The gagging will pass."

She backed off in depth and sucked air in through her nose. Her gag reflex had always been very sensitive.

"If you can't go very deep, it's okay. Use your hand to give me the pressure from the bottom and your mouth to counter it. Roll my balls between your fingers."

She pushed him back slightly and dropped to hers knees so she could get better leverage on what she was doing. The little whimpers, groans and other sounds coming from his mouth as she pleasured him, drove her own desire higher. Wetness coated her pussy. She wished she had a hand free to touch herself. The pressure building between her thighs drove her crazy.

"You're doin' great, darlin'." He pushed his hips toward her face. "A little more suction. Oh yeah. Perfect." She bobbed her head, running her tongue around the tip of his cock as she drove his pleasure higher. "That's it. Okay stop or I'm gonna blow in your mouth and I don't want to. I want to be inside you when I come."

He helped her stand before pushing her back onto the bed and quickly removed the rest of his clothing. The gorgeous body standing in front of her blew her mind. His cock stood long and thick against his abdomen and she wondered again how it would ever fit inside her without tearing her apart.

"I love your breasts. They are fucking gorgeous." He cupped them in both hands, lightly sucking the right and then the left nipple. After he feasted on her breasts for a couple of minutes, he worked his way down her abdomen until he knelt on the floor between her thighs.

"Wait."

"What?"

"What are you gonna do?"

"I want to lick you clean and make you come so hard you see stars."

"But…" He licked the inside of her thigh, stopping with a little nip to the skin. "Ouch."

"This body is mine tonight. No more talking."

He spread her thighs further apart and settled himself *down there*. Embarrassment flushed her cheeks. Her ex had never done this before, which may be part of the reason their love life sucked so badly. Now she knew the difference and…*oh*.

His wet tongue skimmed her outer pussy lips. The rough texture felt heavenly on her pussy as she relaxed into the comforter and let Joel do what he wanted. Fire built her in pelvis. Need scorched her body, flushing her skin to a pale pink. Blood pounded in her ears. The wet slide reached her clit and her hips lifted off the bed. His hand pushed her back down as he flicked his tongue over the hard nub.

"Oh God."

"Come for me, Mesa."

Heat crawled up her legs. Her pelvis burned. Blood rushed in her veins to the one spot he continued to lick. The moment he sucked her clit between his lips, she exploded, screaming his name in the heat of passion she'd never felt before.

"Very nice, baby." Two of his fingers pushed into her pussy. "You're beautiful when you come. Shall we try for another?"

"Another?" she squeaked, exhausted from the first one.

"You can do it again. I know you can."

The two dangerous digits in her pussy felt like heaven and hell at the same time. He shoved them in and out in a slow, taunting rhythm that she found had her blood pounding again in a few short minutes. Surely she couldn't come again so soon?

His tongue returned to her clit doing quick figure eights. His fingers continued their movement and the next thing she knew, she exploded again without much warning this time. No heat in her legs, no tingling in her pussy, nothing to warn her of the impending blast.

"Oh God!" she screamed. "Joel!"

As she slowly returned to awareness, she realized he'd moved from between her thighs to hover over her. His latex covered cock nudged at her opening.

"Are you ready for me?"

"You're so big."

"It'll fit, darlin'. You are so wet, it'll slide right in. Open for me."

She pulled her thighs further apart, tensing as he pushed the head of his cock inside.

"Relax. I won't hurt you."

The slow glide of his cock felt amazing. Her muscles relaxed as he slowly stretched her to take him. "Holy shit, you feel fantastic. More."

"Your wish is my command."

Within moments, he had fully filled her and she had her legs wrapped around his hips. "I need more, Joel."

He chuckled. "There isn't any more, Mesa. You've got all of me, darlin'."

"No. I mean you need to move more." She raised her hips to take him deeper.

"Ah. That I can do, babe." He shifted his hips, dragging his cock from her pussy and then snapping his hips to slam his cock into her.

"Yes, ah God, yes. Do that again." She fisted the comforter beneath her in her hands. Lord, she needed this. Every slide, every movement, every touch brought her higher and higher. He bent over to take her nipple into his mouth. The moan escaping from her lips sounded primal. He growled low in his throat as he continued to pump into her, practically scooting her across the bed. His fingers dug into the fleshy part of her hips. She'd probably have bruises there in the morning but she didn't care. She wanted this with him so badly.

She could taste him on her tongue.

She struggled into a sitting position so she could be closer.

"You okay?"

"Fantastic. Don't stop. I just want to taste your skin." She ran her tongue over the ridges of his chest. His right nipple tempted her so she tongued it and then sucked it between her lips.

He continued to pound into her flesh. The pretzel maneuver felt like wave after wave of sensation breaking over her. Her climax hovered on the edges of her consciousness. She reached for the stars as the final moment crested her mind, throwing her into a spiral of sensation as he groaned her name.

"God, Mesa." He panted. "That was…"

"Awesome?"

"Stupendous. I've never come so hard in my life. I think I lost consciousness there for a second."

"I'm glad."

"Nothin' like makin' an impression, babe."

"And take a little piece of your heart with me?"

Chapter Seven

Her stomach felt like she swallowed a rock. *Not a good thing to say right after sex.* "I'm kidding!"

"Don't do that! You scared the hell out of me." He slowly eased from inside her before he went to dispose of the condom in the bathroom. "Do you need to wash up?"

"Yeah. I'm kind of sticky." She sat up and brushed the hair back from her forehead. Watching him walk away was almost better than watching him walk toward her. The man had a body like a Greek god. He even had a real six-pack!

"Want me to bring you a washcloth or do you want to use the restroom?"

"I better use the bathroom."

"It's all yours," he said with a sweep of his hand.

Even flaccid, his cock seemed huge. *Damn!*

"Do you want to stay here tonight or do you want to go back to the lodge?"

"Either is fine with me. I don't want to crowd you. I know how guys get."

He stopped her at the bathroom door with a hand on her bare shoulder. She felt a little self-conscious standing in front of him completely naked, even though they'd just had mind-blowing sex. "Mesa, I know this is supposed to be casual and all, but I would love for you to stay here and sleep in my arms."

She tossed back her hair and replied, "Then I will. I would love to sleep snuggled up to you."

"Good. Would you like something to drink? I have soda, milk, water, beer…just name it."

"A diet soda would be good if you have one. If not, regular is fine."

"One soda, coming right up." He raised an eyebrow and glanced down at her. "I imagine you didn't bring anything to sleep in so you can use one of my shirts if you like."

"Thanks."

He grabbed a T-shirt from the drawer and handed it to her. "No underwear."

"Huh? Why not?"

"I might want to ravish you again before mornin'."

"Oh. Well then. I'm game." She reached up and kissed him on the lips. "I've gotta get it while the gettin' is good, ya know."

He frowned slightly before he spun on his heels and disappeared down the hallway. His nice, rounded tush caught her attention. He didn't even bother to put anything on before he went into the other room for something to drink. *Now there is a man who is comfortable in his own skin.* She went inside and shut the door to get cleaned up. She definitely wasn't comfortable with her body even if he said he liked it. The mirror showed high color on her cheeks, full lips, red from the pressure of his, whisker burn on her chest and neck from his five o'clock shadow, and a sparkle in her eyes she hadn't seen there in a long time. Joel was good for her. Too bad it wasn't a permanent thing.

She found a washcloth on the counter to clean away the stickiness between her thighs.

"I don't keep a lot of food around here since we take meals at the lodge house," he shouted from the kitchen.

"It's fine. I'm not really hungry anyway," she said, coming out the door of the bathroom.

"I have some snack stuff, if you'd like. Chips, pretzels, popcorn."

"Nah, I'm good." Now, she pulled the comforter down to the end of the bed and crawled beneath the sheet. She frowned. She hadn't thought about what side of the bed he slept on. Would it make a difference? The only man she'd ever slept with on a regular basis was her ex.

"Here," he said, stopping by her side to hand her the soda can.

"I'm okay here, right?"

"You're perfect." He leaned down and kissed her. "Don't be surprised if you end up in the middle. I usually do."

"Are you a snuggler?"

"I guess. I don't have women here very often."

"Really? I'm surprised."

"Why?" he asked, going around to the other side and sliding under the sheet.

"I would think you would have a lot of women. That's all." She sipped from the can before she set it on the nightstand.

"Not really."

"Well, I'm a snuggler, so for tonight, you get to snuggle."

He smiled and wrapped his arm around her shoulders as she settled down along his left side. Her head rested nicely against his chest. His heart pounded in her ear. The hair on his chest tickled her chin, making her giggle.

"What's so funny?"

"Your hair is tickling me."

"You are ticklish?" He slid his hand up her side and curled his fingers into her ribs.

Giggling, she squirmed against him. "Shit. No! Don't tickle me, please? I'm terribly ticklish. Remember at the bar?"

"I'll quit if you give me a kiss."

"All right! No...tickling." She quickly pecked him on the mouth.

"Not good enough." He tickled her again as she squealed.

"Okay!" She grabbed his face on both sides and lip locked his mouth. She pushed her tongue between his lips, tangling with his own. The moan escaping him did nothing to cool the kiss she took deeper still, pressing her breasts against his chest. He never got redressed after the bout of lovemaking earlier, leaving her the ability to graze his body with her fingertips. The muscles beneath her hands drove her desire higher. She wanted to feel him over her, in her, surrounding her until they both came apart at the seams.

Mesa pushed him down on his back and crawled over him, wanting to take in every inch of his body on her way down. Sex wasn't something she enjoyed much with her ex. Moderation and tolerance had become her mantra with him, but she knew with Joel, there would be no tolerating. She needed to be involved in having sex with him. She ran her tongue along his jaw to his ear, nibbling it between her teeth for a moment.

"You're so fucking hot, Mesa," he whispered between panting breaths. Goose bumps rose on his skin following the trail of her fingers.

"You're pretty hot yourself, cowboy. I wanna lick you all over." She ran her tongue across his chest, stopping to nip at the tips of his nipples. Were his sensitive, too? She whipped the T-shirt over her head and tossed it to the side of the bed.

"God, you're drivin' me nuts."

"Good. I don't want to be horny all by myself."

His cock lay hard between them against her stomach, pulsating with life, just waiting to bring her to ecstasy again.

"Oh, hell no." He surged up and flipped her onto her back.

He tasted her breasts, licked at her stomach and then positioned himself between her thighs, spreading her to accommodate the breadth of his shoulders. He dove in, taking no prisoners on his way to bringing her to orgasm within a matter of moments. Her ears burned as the blood rushed to her head before it quickly centered in her pelvis. Her clit throbbed with every beat of her heart, but wasn't letting up. He licked and sucked until she screamed his name on a hoarse cry of delight.

He kissed his way back up her body until he reached her mouth. "I love to make you come."

"I was supposed to be seducing you. Not the other way around."

"I wanna fuck you."

"Good. I want you to."

He hopped down from the bed after a quick kiss to her lips. A frown wrinkled the skin between her eyes as she watched him retrieve his belt. *Holy shit!*

"Ever been tied up?"

"Can't say that I have. What are you gonna do with the belt?"

"No beating you with it, although welts on your ass would turn me inside out." He looped the belt around her wrists and secured them loosely to the headboard. "Roll over onto your stomach and get up on your knees.

I'm gonna fuck you hard from behind." He grinned rolling the condom he retrieved from the nightstand drawer over his rigid cock. "Ever had a man in your ass?"

She swallowed the lump clogging her throat and shook her head, unable to speak through the fear making her heart pound in her chest. Her ex tried it once and the pain had almost killed her. Terror made her shudder uncontrollably.

"What's wrong, darlin'? I won't do anything you don't want, but you look terrified."

"I can't," she whispered.

"Can't?"

"I won't, I mean. You won't do that will you?"

"Take your ass, you mean?"

She nodded furiously.

"Honey, I can see the thought scares you to death. I wouldn't do anything to hurt you. If you don't want to try it, then we won't. Obviously you've had a bad experience with it or something to make you so afraid." He skimmed his hand over her breasts bringing the peaks to hard little points. "You like a little pain with your sex, but I won't do anything beyond what you can handle."

"Thank you."

"Relax, darlin'." He helped her roll over, rubbing her shoulders turning them to mush in the process. He kissed her butt cheeks before he smacked each one in turn just enough to make her wet. His fingers probed at her pussy, driving two in deep as he finger fucked her for several minutes. She moaned as she closed her eyes. Her thighs spread of their own accord. She had no will to do anything but let him to whatever he wanted to her.

He helped her rise up on her knees, bracing herself on her folded arms. "Fuck me, Joel."

"Oh I intend to, darlin'."

She felt his cock nudge at her pussy and groaned as he sank balls deep inside her.

"God, you're tight, babe."

"You feel amazing."

"Hold on, honey. I'm gonna fuck you hard."

He set up a steady, ass thumping rhythm, throwing her head over heels into a screaming orgasm almost immediately, but he didn't stop. He continued to pound into her, shaking the mattress on the frame and banging the headboard against the wall.

"Ah God, Joel!"

"You can come again. I know you can. Squeeze me with that hot pussy of yours."

The second she exploded into another orgasm, she heard him lose control. He growled low in his throat and lost the rhythmic pounding of his hips to a completely uncoordinated cadence as he shot his sperm into the condom.

"You're gonna be the death of me."

"Nah, you're a man. You can handle it." She giggled as she smacked him on the butt cheek the moment he let her out of her bindings.

"Hey. I'm supposed to do the ass warmin'."

"What you aren't a switch?"

He withdrew from her and sat up on the side of the bed with a puzzled look on his gorgeous face. "What do you know about being a switch?"

"Not a lot. I've read some romances with BDSM in it. I don't know how much of it is true, but it interests me."

"Does it, now. Hmm. Maybe we need to explore a bit more while you're here."

"So much for not ravishing the guests."

He frowned and reached for his pants. "Don't get me wrong, we have to be careful, but there's a lot of fun to be had. We just can't let anyone know what's happening between us."

"We have to keep this a secret? Seriously?" she asked, pulling the sheet up to cover her breasts.

"We had some good sex, Mesa. Nothin' more. If we tell anyone in my family, especially my mother, she'll have us married and havin' kids before the end of the week," he said from the bathroom. "Besides, the fuck was almost the best I've ever had."

"Almost?" she snapped, fury rushing through her at his offhanded compliment, then slamming her back down with it being almost the best he's ever had. *God, I'm such an idiot!*

"Easy, Mesa. I didn't mean anythin' by it," he replied, coming out with his pants on but not buttoned.

"Yeah. Tonight was a test. Just a quick fuck, with the potential for more during my stay. I get it, Joel." She grabbed her clothes from the floor, struggling to snap herself back into her bra with about as much grace as an octopus.

"What are you doin', darlin'?" He touched her shoulder but she shrugged him off.

"Don't darlin' me. I want you to take me back to the lodge or I'll walk."

"No you won't."

"Yes, I will. Don't tell me what to do. You might be able to dominate me in bed, but I'm my own person and I don't take kindly to men telling me what to do. I have a mind of my own. I can make my own decisions." She flipped her hair out of the collar of her shirt as she slipped her tennis shoes on her feet. "Are you gonna take me back?"

"Fine," he growled, tugging the T-shirt she'd been wearing on.

His magnificent chest disappeared from view. She bit her lips to keep from moaning at the loss. "Fine."

He slid on a pair of flip-flops, then stood there impatiently tapping his foot. Without another word, she headed for the door with him on her heels. So much for a great evening spent in the arms of a hot cowboy. Yeah, they'd had great sex but the minute things got a little testy, they were at each other's throats. He wouldn't tell his family they were sleeping together because he didn't want his mother playing matchmaker. Well, she didn't want that either. He didn't have to make it sound like a huge mistake for them to make love. Now she felt used and cheap.

Several moments later, they pulled up in front of the lodge. She didn't even wait for him to come around and open the door. She just hopped out on her own, slammed the truck door and headed for the house. Joel sprayed gravel as he backed out and then sped off down the driveway.

Tears rolled down her cheeks. *God, I've been such an idiot where he's concerned. Good lookin' cowboy is all it takes. I'm all over it and him.*

"Great job, Mesa. Sleep with the man. What a fuckin' waste of time."

The door to the lodge opened in front of her, and then closed as a cowboy she didn't recognize came out.

"Ma'am." He tipped his hat and walked down the stairs. She shook her head as she turned to see where he was going, but he'd disappeared.

"All right. I'm gonna have to ask someone. This is getting too weird for me. Doors open and close without anyone around, voices and knocks on my door when there is no one there, people disappearing without a trace."

She opened the door and walked inside. The house was quiet. No one stirred. She headed across the dining room toward the stairs to go to her room when goose bumps started to rise on her arms. The air turned colder. She glanced back at the door she'd just come through in time to see it open, and then closed on its own.

Just a little freaked out, she ran up the stairs. She fumbled with the key to her room for a moment before sprinting through the door and slamming it sharply behind her.

* * * *

Joel stepped through the door of his cabin, flinging the keys to his truck against the wall. Frustration, anger and just a little bit of fear raced through him. *How could things have gotten so screwed up? What the hell did I say to piss her off so badly?*

"I said it was good sex. What the hell more does she want? I certainly can't let my family know we slept together. Mom would have a coronary or have us in front of a preacher as soon as she could arrange it." He tossed off his flip-flops and dropped onto the sofa. His cell phone jingled in his pocket. "Yeah," he answered after he'd pulled it out.

"What's up, bro?"

"What do you want, Jacob?"

"I thought I'd check in with you. I thought I saw you drop Mesa off at the lodge."

"I did."

"And?"

"What? She's majorly fuckin' pissed at me for some damn reason."

"What the hell did you do?"

"I don't fuckin' know. That's just it." He raked his fingers through his hair. "I mean we had great sex. I thought everythin' was great. She got a burr under her blanket and insisted I take her back."

"Tell me what you said."

"I told her we couldn't let anyone know what's happened between us."

"She said, we have to keep this a secret and I said yes. We had some good sex, Mesa. Nothin' more. If we tell anyone in my family, especially my mother, she'll have us married and havin' kids before the end of the week. Then I said, besides, the fuck was almost the best I've ever had."

"Holy shit! Are you fuckin' dense man?"

"What?"

"You told her she was *almost* the best. You might as well tell her she's okay in the sack. You never tell a woman they are almost the best you ever had. Then you told her you couldn't tell anyone you'd been together."

"Well, we can't. Mom would have a cow. You know she would."

"Seriously, Joel. Don't you think the rest of us have fucked a guest before?"

"You have?"

"Hell yeah. Remember the set of twins who visited last year in late summer. Blonde, big boobs?"

"Tiffany and Trena?"

"Yeah, I guess. Hell, I don't even remember their names, but I had both of them. At once."

"What? Are you fuckin' kiddin' me?"

"No and Mom knows. The girls weren't quiet about it the next day. They were discussing it in the dining room. Of course, they couldn't tell any of us apart so I doubt they could even say which one of us fucked them."

"I know it wasn't me."

"I know who it was, dipwad. I might have been a little drunk, but I sure remember fuckin' both of them."

"I've never had two at once."

"It's an experience." He coughed in the phone. "I assume you enjoyed yourself with Mesa."

"Hell yeah. She was fantastic, but I doubt she'll even talk to me the rest of the time she's here."

"I don't think she'll hold a grudge."

"Why?"

"Because she's hung up on you, dude."

"I've only known her a couple of days."

"Yeah, but it doesn't mean shit when a heart gets involved. I've seen the way she looks at you."

"We'll see tomorrow, I guess."

Their conversation wrapped up a few minutes later when he clicked off the phone. *Did I really screw things up so bad with Mesa that she won't talk to me again? I hope not. I really like her a lot and in bed? Holy fuck!*

He grabbed a beer from the refrigerator before he walked into his room and stripped off his clothes. The sheets felt cool to his heated skin as he slid beneath them. The light slipped off with a twist of his fingers.

Moonlight streamed in through the open window as a cool breeze tickled across his skin. The scent of Mesa drifted to him on the air so he rolled over and pulled the pillow her head had been on, to his face. He couldn't quite place the flowery scent, but he knew it belonged uniquely to her. He'd smelled it on her hair when he'd been buried deep inside her pussy. His cock hardened at the mere thought of her wrapped around him. He groaned, fisting his cock in his hand. There would be no getting any sleep tonight with his raging hard-on. It had been a long time since he'd been this turned on by a woman...any woman. He pumped his fist several times while he imagined Mesa's hot pussy surrounding him, scalding him with her heat.

In no time at all, he felt the pull of his balls to his groin and the tingling sensation signaling the inevitable release. Cum shot out the end of his dick, splashing the white substance across his stomach. He moaned and slumped against the pillows. *Damn.* He swung his legs over the side of the bed as he let his head drop in exhaustion. For several moments he sat there inhaling lungsful of air, trying to calm his racing heart. Getting himself off like that after already coming with Mesa, almost hurt, but it was better than trying to sleep hard as a damn rock. He stumbled to the bathroom to wash the cum from his abdomen before he succumbed to sleep.

Now he might be able to actually sleep, although he feared dreams of her would bother him through the night whether he wanted them to or not.

Chapter Eight

She needed to talk to Joel or Nina or Joel's dad. The noises of the couple arguing again woke her at two in the morning. The knock sounded on her door shortly afterward but she feared opening it to find no one on the other side. Things seemed too strange and she needed to find out what was going on.

A light misty rain fell from the gray skies. *It gets cloudy in Texas?* Thunder rumbled in the distance. Goose bumps rose on her arms. Thunderstorms bothered her some, but there was electricity in the air trying to fight for substance like nothing she'd ever felt before.

The breakfast bell clanged downstairs signaling the return of the crowd staying at the ranch for the next meal. She dreaded facing Joel or his family after the night before. Sure, they'd had sex. At least for her it had been phenomenal sex. Apparently for him, it was just okay. She should have known. A guy like him didn't usually have anything to do with women like her. The plain, a little plump, and the nothing-to-write-home-to-mom-about type girl didn't get the gorgeous, hunky cowboy. It just didn't happen except in her novels.

After she slipped on her shoes, she grabbed her small backpack and locked the door. She glanced down the hall to the left and right almost expecting to see someone there. Nothing.

The aroma of bacon and eggs drifted to her nose. Her stomach rumbled in protest. She took the stairs begrudgingly as she prepared herself for the inevitable rush she felt every time she saw Joel.

The entire family sat at their usual table waiting for the guests to get their plates. She glanced down the long expanse to notice one empty chair. Joel wasn't there.

Where was he? Surely he didn't feel guilty about the way they fought last night?

She got into the line for her food and chatted with an older woman about the weather.

"Too bad it's raining today. We wanted to go riding."

"You can still ride even in the wet weather, although it's not as comfortable."

"We are city slickers. We don't do wet leather or wet jeans," the woman answered with a smile. "We're living out our fantasies of cowboys with all these hunky men around, but I think today will just be a sit-around-and-drool day."

"Anyone special you are drooling over?"

"Well the triplets are just awesome. Can you imagine having the attention of all three at once?"

"I don't think I could handle all three at once."

"I'd sure give it a try," the woman replied, giggling under her breath as she glanced at the table.

The door burst open with a gust of wind. Mesa gasped as she glanced at the door and the silhouette of the man outlined. The width of his shoulders. The breadth of his chest. The ruffle of hair at his neck. The black Stetson shading his face. Even though she couldn't see his face, she knew him. She knew his body like she knew her own...by the touch of her hands.

Joel.

He pulled the door shut behind him, blocking the gust of wind whipping through and blowing rain in from outside. His eyes never left hers as he walked up to her and smiled before moving down to the table where the coffee sat.

"Interesting." The woman she'd been talking to moved away.

Mesa's gaze never left Joel.

Once he had his coffee, he turned toward her, sipped the dark brew, and gave her a sexy wink.

Well, apparently he thinks I'm not pissed at him anymore. She didn't respond except for a frown as she grabbed her plate.

Instead of sitting in her normal spot next to him at the family table, she chose a table with a bunch of women. "Mind if I sit with you ladies?"

"Of course not. Please," a large, older woman replied. "There's always room for one more."

"Are you ladies here for a few days?"

"Yes. We love the ranch life and wanted to experience it for ourselves. You know instead of always reading about it, we wanted to see it."

"Oh? You ladies read?"

"Of course we do," a petite blonde answered. "We are a book club."

"Wonderful! What do you ladies like to read?"

A redhead to her left giggled. "Romance, of course. Hot cowboys." She glanced at the family table with wide eyes. "You know. Like they are."

"I know exactly what you mean." She took several bites. "Who are your favorite authors?"

The ladies glanced at each other and said in unison, "Mesa West."

"Really?"

The lady to her right clapped and said, "We heard you were here visiting when you posted on your Facebook status. We would love for you to sign some of our books we brought."

"Of course!"

"Many of us live in San Antonio and were disappointed you weren't at the book signing yesterday, so we drove out here to have some one on one time with you if you don't mind."

"Of course I don't mind. You ladies have made my day. I would love to sit and chat with you for a while about books."

"Is Troy going to get his own story?" a brunette asked from the end of the table as she clapped excitedly. "I absolutely loved him in Trouble in Cowboy Boots."

"I did too, and yes, he's definitely getting his own story."

"When?"

"Soon, I hope. I'm here trying to get some inspiration for a new series."

"Wow! Really?"

She nodded as she glanced at Joel from the corner of her eye. One eyebrow went up above his left eye. *Damn the man.*

Excited chatter enveloped her while the women shot her question after question about her characters, stories, and inspiration. Where did she come up with her stories? Were there real men who inspired her cowboys? The more questions, the more she lost herself in the enthusiasm of her readers.

The crowd came and went from the dining room while they continued to talk. Several moments ago, Joel had walked by, brushing her shoulders with his fingers in a gesture mistaken for innocence, but she knew different. He was ramping up her need for him with the simple touch.

"Are you seeing the cute one who just walked by?" the redhead asked as Joel walked out the door, taking his scent with him.

"Seeing? No. He's just been helping me with research about ranch life and cowboying while I'm here. We've only known each other a couple of days."

"He seems taken with you."

"Me?" She laughed ruefully knowing there wouldn't ever be anything more than a quick tumble between the sheets with Joel. "Yeah, no. His kind doesn't get taken with women like me."

"You're a beautiful girl. I don't know why you say such things. We love you."

"Aw, thank you, ladies." The kitchen workers eyed them. "I think we should clean up our dishes and maybe move into the main lodge to continue our discussions. They want to get things ready for lunch in a few hours."

The group picked up their dishes and deposited them in the washbasin before they retreated to the main lodge area where the fireplace and large bookcases where located. There were several couches all arranged in a semi-circle in front of the cold fireplace where everyone could chat without bothering anyone else. Mesa took a chair at the center of the group, fielding the rapid-fire questions the women threw at her. She loved chatting with readers and being the only author in the room, she could let their enthusiasm surround her, lift her spirits, and give her muse a quick kick in the butt.

The women spent the next couple of hours pounding her with questions, laughing at some of her responses, and just generally having a good time.

"I totally appreciate you ladies making the trip out here just to see me. I'm thrilled you came. You've all made my day."

"Thank you for spending a few hours out of your busy schedule to chat with us, Mesa. It's been fantastic and I'm sure we'll all be buying your next book the moment it hits the shelves."

"I hope you get some great inspiration from your cowboy friend."

"Yeah, me too. He's been fabulous so far, but now I need to track him down and ask him a few questions so if you ladies will excuse me."

"Of course. Thank you again and we'll see you at the next conference. You'll be at the one in Dallas, right?"

"Yes, ma'am. The one in a couple of months is my next stop."

"Awesome." The ladies waved goodbye as they made their way back toward the main lodge door, leaving her in silence.

Nina came out of her office with a big smile on her face. "You made their day."

"Thanks but it was more like the other way around. They made mine. I really needed the boost to my morale."

"Oh?" she asked, taking one of the empty seats.

"I've just been really down in the dumps lately, questioning my writing."

"You're a fabulous writer, Mesa. I don't see why you're questioning yourself. I got two of your books yesterday after you were here and I haven't been able to put them down since I started reading them. My husband finally forced me to turn off the lights last night at four in the morning."

Mesa laughed. "Thank you. That's the best compliment a writer can get."

"You're welcome."

She looked at Nina with a frown. "Can I ask you a couple of questions about the ranch? You know, from a woman's perceptive?"

"Certainly."

For the next hour, Mesa picked Nina's brain for information on the ranch life, raising nine boys and life in general with a bunch of men.

"I need to ask you a couple more questions about the ranch."

"All right."

"First of all, do you believe in ghosts?"

"Yes, I do. We have a few on the ranch."

"Really?"

"Yes. The main lodge used to be a bordello. That's the reason for its size. It's been added onto over the years, but it used to be a bar and whore house. The upstairs bedrooms were where the women took their men." She laughed. "Of course, we've cleaned them up since then."

"Wow."

"It has a very interesting history."

"What kinds of ghosts are here?"

"A cowboy. A couple who visit upstairs. A saloon girl and a few kids who run the ranch. You can hear them giggling outside sometimes."

"You have so many!"

"It's been a lively place for a long time." She tilted her head to the side. "Why so many questions? Have you seen them?"

"I think so." She took a deep breath and let it out slowly. "A cowboy at least. Someone has knocked on my door twice now in the middle of the night. I've also heard arguing in the next room."

"The cowboy you've seen is a regular around here. The best we can figure is he used to work the ranch many years ago as a wrangler and never left. We haven't been able to pinpoint his identity exactly."

"And the fighting couple?"

"Probably one of the cowboys and his girl fighting in the room up there."

"It sounds like he slaps her."

"Yep. That's them. They get kind of noisy sometimes. If you bang on the wall and tell them to knock it off, it goes away. Don't worry about the knocking. If there were an emergency, we would shout through the door. We haven't been able to figure it out yet, but it happens frequently."

"Kind of creepy, don't you think?"

"If it bothers you, I can move you to one of the outside cabins. They aren't haunted."

"I'm okay, but don't be surprised if your ghosts end up in one of my books."

Nina laughed. "I would love it. They are characters for sure. Have you seen the saloon girl?"

"No. Just the cowboy. Last night when I came back from Joel's, he…" *Oh shit.*

Nina patted her hand and said, "Don't worry about it, Mesa. I heard you come in last night and the roar of Joel's truck out in the yard. I looked out the window as he tore out of here. His truck has a distinctive sound."

Mesa felt the heat of a blush rushing into her cheeks. Her heart pounded in her ears as she sought to apologize for breaking the rules. "I'm sorry, Nina. I know you have a strict rule about the guys and guests, but…"

"It's fine, honey. If you and Joel are attracted to each other, it's okay. I just don't want the boy's going through guests on a regular basis, like water down the stream. You know how men are."

"Yes, I do."

"Did y'all have a fight last night? I thought I heard the truck door slam."

"A little bit."

"Would you like to talk about it?"

She blew out a breath. Talking to his mother about problems with Joel didn't seem like a good idea, but she really needed someone to talk to. She wasn't really close to her siblings or her mother, but Nina seemed to understand these kinds of things. It didn't take long at all for the entire story to spill from her lips. Nina murmured between her sentences in a soothing voice meant to calm her. "It'll be all right, honey. He's a man. Men tend to get pigheaded sometimes and trust me, I've seen it more than I care to with my boys. They take after their father that way."

Mesa laughed. She could totally see the stubbornness in Nina too, but she didn't want to insult her hostess. "Thank you for talking with me."

"Let me give you a little piece of advice. Avoid Joel for the day. You're going to be here for a few more days. You'll have plenty of time to talk to him. Go for a walk. Write. Read for your own pleasure for a change. I bet you don't read very often without worrying about your own books."

"True."

"I saw the way he touched you on his way out the door. He's a very possessive guy when it comes to women. It was his way of marking you, to let his brothers know you're taken."

"Seriously?"

"Yes, ma'am." Nina nodded with a smile. "Y'all are cute together. I haven't seen him act this way toward a woman before."

"I'm so not his type though."

"Sure you are! He's never been into skinny women. You're just his type." She patted Mesa's hand and then stood. "I've got some work to do. You enjoy your day and don't worry about Joel. He'll come find you either later tonight after supper or tomorrow."

"Thank you, Nina. You've been a huge help."

"You're welcome, honey. I've enjoyed having you here."

"Oh. I'll get your dress and shoes back to you later this afternoon. Would it be okay if I did some laundry? I didn't bring very many clothes with me on this trip and I'm about out of clean underwear."

"Of course. You know where the laundry facilities are. Use whatever you need. There is soap and dryer sheets on the shelf."

"You've been such a great hostess. You can bet I'll be singing your praises and those of the ranch on every social network I'm on when I get home."

"Word of mouth is the best advertising we can ask for. Thank you." She nodded again before she headed back for her office, leaving Mesa to sit alone in front of the fireplace contemplating her thoughts.

Maybe Nina is right. I should avoid Joel until he comes looking for me. She bit her lip as trepidation rush through her. *But what if he doesn't come looking? I'll feel like a total fool.*

The smile he gave her earlier brought back memories of their night together. His hands on her flesh. His lips taking what he wanted. His body covering hers as he took her to heights of ecstasy she'd never felt before. Did he do the same thing with every woman he made love to? She shook her head. Surely it was that way with any man who knew how to make love to a woman, right?

Remember your ex, her head said before she could think any further. He couldn't fuck if he tried. All he knew how to do was stick it in, pump a few times and flop down on top of her. Then he actually had the nerve to ask if it was good for her. Well nope, it wasn't. It sucked!

Now with Joel, wow!

"Okay, enough thoughts of Joel. I've got some writing to do."

* * * *

Joel wound his horse around a boulder keeping an eye out for snakes as he checked the fence for breaks and the cattle for strays. His thoughts weren't on his job though. He wanted to see Mesa. He knew he'd pissed her off last night with his casual remark about their lovemaking, but he really didn't want to give her the impression it might turn into something more than a quick fuck. Hell, she didn't even live in Texas!

"Yo, Joel!"

He pulled on Jet's reins as Jeremiah rode up on his horse.

"What are you doing out here?"

"I came to find you. Mom was looking for you earlier."

"Oh great."

"Yeah. I'm sure it's something about you coming home with Mesa last night."

"What the fuck? Does everyone know?"

"Of course they do, dumbass. One, you brought her home in your truck with its loud-assed muffler and two, she's staying in the main lodge. Everyone in the place probably heard you bring her home."

Joel tipped his head back on his shoulders and sighed. *Great.* Everyone in the family knew they'd been together without him or her saying a damned word. His mom probably wanted to kill him. "I guess I better go find her."

"Yeah, I would say so. You know how she is. Mom's gonna rip you a new asshole, buddy."

"Great. Thanks for the support, Jeremiah."

"You're welcome, bro."

"Asswipe."

Joel kicked his horse into a slow gallop headed for the barn. Despite the probable indigestion, he wanted this confrontation with his mother over with before supper. *Maybe I can find Mesa while I'm at the house.*

Several minutes later, he rounded the barn for the corral as Jeff came out of the tack room. "Joel? What are you doin' back from ridin' fences?"

"Mom wanted to talk to me if it's any of your business."

"Everything on this ranch is my business. The horses, the cattle, where the hands are…everything."

"I'm not your damned employee, Jeff. What I do is none of your concern no matter whether you think you're in charge or not." He swung down from the saddle, and then began unbuckling the straps. "Besides, what the hell are you doin' in the barn this time of day? Don't you have somethin' to keep you busy besides the barn?"

"I'm checking the feed stock, fucktard."

"Well get busy then, asshole. I've got my own worries."

"Oh? Like fuckin' one of the guests?"

"Blow it out your ass, brother. What I do is none of your damned business. How many times do I have to tell you?"

"One day Dad won't be here and everything will fall on me. I'm not doing anythin' more than what will be expected of me when the time comes."

"Dad isn't going anywhere for a long time, Jeff, so back off. I'll talk to Mom about me and Mesa."

"Keep your hands off the guests."

He pushed against Jeff's chest. "Make me. I can fuck whomever I want to and you can't say a damned thing."

"The hell I can't."

"Enough you two!" shouted his father. "Jeff back off."

"What?"

"I said back off. What happens on this ranch is mine and your mother's concern. We will deal with your brothers. Not you."

"But Dad…"

"But nothing. This is between me, your mother, and Joel."

Joel smirked, earning a growl from his brother as he balled his fists at his sides. He could tell Jeff wanted to kick his ass. Let him try. Jeff might be about the same size as him, but he had a little more bulk to his frame, whereas his brother wasn't quite so muscular.

"In the house, Joel."

"I'm not done with you, Joel," Jeff snarled.

"Fuck you."

"I said in the house," his father snapped, pointing to the main lodge.

As Joel's steps took him toward the lodge, he whistled knowing his father stayed back for a moment to reprimand his eldest brother. Jeff really needed to get laid or something. The guy had a serious stick up his ass the size of a fence post.

He walked inside, relishing the cool interior. The rain hadn't let up all day and he was soaked to the bone. A nice dry change of clothes would be good but he'd have to make a trip back to his place to get them.

"Joel?"

"Yeah, Ma."

"I'm in the office."

"Be right there."

He dragged his feet as he released a heavy sigh. Twenty eight years old, and that tone still sent chills down his spine. With a heavy sigh, he shuffled his feet toward his mother's domain.

"Have a seat," she said the minute he stood in the doorway. "We need to talk."

"Are you gonna wait for Dad?" he asked, sliding into the chair across from her desk. He hadn't felt so put on the spot like this in several years. Not since she'd found out he'd been visiting their neighbor's daughter.

"Your father will be along shortly, I'm sure. But we've already discussed this at length before I went looking for you earlier."

"So what's up?"

"It's you and Mesa, son."

"What about us?"

"So there is an us?"

"Well..."

"No hemhawin' about it. I know you were together last night. I saw her come in and heard you peel out of the driveway, digging up about three quarters of the gravel we laid this summer."

"Sorry, Ma."

"Joel, honey. I'm not mad at you. I like Mesa. I think she's a wonderful girl. The reason for this talk isn't to chew you out for bein' with her. It's so you don't hurt her."

"I don't plan to hurt her, Ma. We're just havin' a bit of fun while she's here."

"That's exactly why I made the rule of you boys not pursing guests." She stood up and paced the room like a cage animal. "I don't want this place getting a reputation for the wild Young boys taking all the single guests to bed."

"It's not like that. Mesa understands."

"Does she? I think she's a nice girl who's been swept off her feet by a handsome cowboy. She doesn't come across as a worldly type woman. She's not one for casual relationships, Joel. What if she does develop feelings for you?"

"Aren't you the least bit worried about me?"

"You're a lover, son, not a fighter although you wouldn't believe it the way you and Jeff were ready to go toe to toe in the barn a few moments ago," his father said, coming into the room.

"And the way you and Joshua went at it the night before last."

"It doesn't matter. Aren't we here to discuss me and Mesa?"

"Yes we are. I want to you stay away from her, Joel," his mother said. "I'm afraid she's gonna get hurt."

"I don't want to hurt her, Ma. She's a friend."

"A friend with benefits?" his dad asked.

Joel pulled off his Stetson, raking his fingers through his hair. "Hell, I don't know what she is. We had fun together. Where it goes from here, I'm not sure. She doesn't even live here. She lives in Los Angeles, for God's sake!"

"What if she moved here?"

"She's not moving here."

"What if she did?"

Joel got up and paced the room now. "I don't know, Ma. I like her a lot. We have a lot in common and she's a wildcat between the sheets, but is there something else there? I don't know."

"Do you want to find out?"

"Sure I would."

"Then ask her to stay."

"What? You can't be serious. She doesn't live here. I told you, she lives in California."

"I understand she lives somewhere else, but she's also a writer who has the ability to be wherever she wants because she's self-employed."

"You've done your homework, Ma."

"Thank you, Joel. I like to know about our guests. We had a nice conversation earlier today."

"You did?"

"Yeah and I think, for the record, she likes you a lot, but she's confused by your actions. You marked her earlier."

He hoped his mother and father understood the confused looked on his face because he didn't have a clue what she meant. "Marked?"

"You ran your fingers along her shoulder on your way out of the lodge this morning. You marked her in front of your brothers, the other males in the room, as your own."

"You've read too much Native American History, Ma."

"So what if I have?" She stopped in front of him. "Honey, I want you happy. If Mesa makes you happy then be my guest, but I like her too and if you hurt that girl, I'm going to kick your ass."

Chapter Nine

The window she stared out of overlooked the back of the lodge house. Her laptop sat in front of her, the cursor blinking mockingly. She had been at it for hours now, the story flowing so rapidly, she could hardly type fast enough. Now, she looked out the window, her mind almost blank.

She could see the comings and goings of several of the boys from her window, but she never saw Joel. With her state of mind, it might be a good thing she didn't. She wanted to get some words on virtual paper before supper.

After several hours of typing, she went back to read what she wrote, realizing the entire book was her trip to the ranch, meeting Joel, and their subsequent love making the night before. Reading it on the screen made her realize how hot the whole night had been and how much she wanted it to happen again.

A heavy sigh rushed from between her lips as she tipped her head back on her shoulders. The cowboy in her book even sounded like Joel.

Joel.

What the hell was she going to do about him? His mother said to avoid him today, which she'd done with regret. She needed to talk to him. Wanted to see him. Would die to taste him.

"Enough. We need to write."

She glanced at the screen, realizing the story stood where her own life stopped at the moment. *What to do from here?*

The supper bell clanged downstairs. She stood, stretching her back until it popped, relieving some of the pressure at her spine from sitting without moving in the hardback chair. Her stomach rumbled reminding her she'd missed lunch. Even though she'd heard the bell earlier, the book wouldn't release her long enough to go eat. Now, she regretted not going even though it would have meant seeing Joel.

Ah, the life of a writer. Caffeine and snacks at the desk. She couldn't remember how many times those things had been her sustenance for days on end while she fought to finish a book before the deadline.

The rumbled of voices downstairs reminded her of supper.

"Well, I can't avoid him for the meal unless I sit somewhere else."

She grabbed her key, opened the door, and shut it before heading down the stairs to join everyone for the evening meal.

Laughter met her ears as she reached the bottom stair and looked out into the expanse of the dining room. The rain had stopped, finally allowing the sun to come out later in the afternoon, lightening everyone's mood. Several women sat at one table laughing and passing around a bottle of wine. They didn't serve liquor at the ranch, but you were welcome to bring your own.

The family sat at their regular table and several of them called out when they noticed her standing in the entryway. She waved before she got in line to get her dinner plate.

Where to sit. Where to sit. She glanced around hoping to find the women from earlier in the group, but no one looked familiar. The book club must have left right after her chat with them. Too bad. She would have enjoyed talking books with them a little longer.

Warm breath tickled her ear, sending goose bumps down her arms. Joel. "No escape, little bird. You've been avoiding me."

"No I haven't. I've been writing." Well, both were the truth. She had been writing, but also avoiding him like his mother suggested.

"Good. I'm glad you've been busy. I've missed you today. It was kind of lonely riding by myself. I thought you were going to ride with me."

She swallowed hard. "I have to strike while the iron is hot."

"Oh, the iron is hot, mi'lady."

"I thought you didn't want to see me."

"I never said I didn't want to see you and now that my whole family knows about us, we don't have to keep it a secret."

"Your whole damned family!" Everyone turned to look at them as embarrassment flushed her cheeks with heat. "Great. Just fucking fabulous," she grumbled under her breath.

"Sorry, darlin', but apparently they all heard you come in last night and me peel out of the driveway."

The young woman dishing up the roast beef winked as she placed the meat on her plate. The next woman smiled while she put mashed potatoes next to the meat. *Just fucking great. Everyone does know about Joel bringing me back to the ranch. They couldn't know we slept together, but they are all assuming as much from their behavior.*

"I don't want to talk about it."

"We need to, Mesa. It's important."

"Leave me alone, Joel. I'm here for research and to write, not hook up with a hot-ass cowboy for a few nights."

"Hot-ass?"

She exhaled sharply, rolled her eyes and headed toward the opposite end of the dining room. One of the tables near the door was empty so she took it. She didn't want company tonight anyway. The moment she sat down, the bench across from her scraped the floor as Joel took the seat on the other side.

"Why aren't you eating at the family table?"

"Because I want to talk to you."

"I thought we'd said everything there needed saying. You didn't want your family to know about us. Well, we apparently took care of that last night. There isn't any need to further our association. You got what you wanted. A lonely, plump, not so attractive woman to fall into bed with you. You've marked your bedpost, I'm sure. One more in the sack for Joel. Great. Good for you. You can chalk it up to experience because I'm done."

"Why are you so upset?"

"Because I don't like being used, Joel, and I feel like you did nothing more than use me."

"Didn't you use me a little, too? I mean, we had a good time last night. Obviously, you needed me and I needed you. We both got what we wanted."

"We both got…you seriously think that?"

"Yeah."

Anger rushed through her so fast her head began to feel funny. Like she'd been swimming and stayed under too long. Her ears burned as she glanced down at the plate in front of her. Not wanting to ruin her own dinner, she grabbed the edge of his plate and unceremoniously dumped the contents of his dinner into his lap.

She grabbed her own plate and walked over to a table where a couple sat alone talking quietly. *Let him stew.*

Watching from the corner of her eye, she saw him slowly scrap the roast beef, gravy and mashed potatoes from his lap back on to the plate. Once his lap was sufficiently cleaned off, he dumped it into the washbasin where the dirty plates go, and stomped out of the lodge, slamming the door behind him.

That should teach him not to mess with me.

Mesa slowly put the spoon in her mouth, avoiding eye contact with any of his family. The whole dining room finally resumed talking after the blow up, but they seemed quiet and subdued. Well, it didn't matter whether their whole affair made the rounds of the entire ranch. She wasn't staying there much longer anyway. Soon she would be home, in her own bed, curled with up her cat and her half-gallon of chocolate chip ice cream eating her cares away. The situation would be a distant memory just like them making love. Would she forget? She hoped, in time.

Several minutes later, Joel returned in clean clothes but he didn't get another plate of food. He walked straight up behind her, grabbed her hand, and forced her to her feet.

"What the hell are you doing?"

"We're having this out, right now."

"I'm not going anywhere with you."

"Yes, you are."

He tugged her along, practically dragging her up the stairs to her room. "Key." She stubbornly narrowed her eyes. "Give me the key, Mesa, or I'll strip you bare until I find it, right here in the hall."

"Fine," she growled, pulling it from her front jean pocket and handing it to him. "I don't want you in my room."

"Too fuckin' bad, baby doll, because I intend to make you listen to me."

He opened the door and literally pushed her inside before he slammed it closed. "Strip."

"Excuse me?"

"I said strip. Do it now."

"I'm not taking my clothes—"

He grabbed her T-shirt and pulled it over her head. "I'll do it for you then."

"What the hell, Joel!"

"Take it off."

"No."

"Fine." He grabbed her pants, popped the button and shoved them down around her ankles so fast, she didn't know what hit her.

Within seconds, she stood in nothing but her bra and panties. Desire pooled in her belly. *How fucking sick is that!* "All right. You have me in nothing but my bra and underwear. I'm not stripping down to nothing. Take it or leave it."

"All right. You can keep them unless you start arguing with me again. If you do, I'm taking those too."

"Fuck you."

"Only if you ask nicely."

"You son of a bitch. Why can't you just leave me alone? I don't want anything more to do with you.

You're a user, Joel, and I don't want to be part of your game anymore."

"Stop. Just stop, Mesa. Listen to yourself? Do you hear what you're saying?"

Tears rolled down her cheeks unchecked. She didn't want to cry but she didn't have a choice. His cavalier attitude hurt her heart. When did she start caring about this rotten asshole? "I hate you."

"No you don't," he whispered, stopping in front of her to wipe the tears from her cheeks. "That's our problem. Neither of us hates the other, but we don't know what else to call it." He kissed her cheeks before he brushed his lips against hers. "God, you taste like Heaven and Hell wrapped up in a single package. What am I gonna do with you, darlin'?"

He kissed her again, pushing his tongue into her mouth tentatively like he was waiting for her to give into her feelings and return the kiss. *Why am I giving into this, him? God, I hate myself for wanting him.*

She grabbed fistfuls of the front of his shirt and pulled the edges apart, buttons pinged off each surface they touched in their flight across the room. He lifted his head, staring down into her eyes, his crystal clear blue eyes bright with lust.

"That's it, Mesa. Take what you want." He pulled at his belt buckle, unhooking it from the loops as she worked his shirt from the waistband of his jeans.

His jeans and boxers hit the floor while he toed out of his boots. She worked frantically at the clasp of her bra until it came free. The next second her panties hit the floor at their feet and he grabbed her around the waist to fling her onto the bed.

"I'm gonna fuck you hard."

"Too much talking." She pressed her mouth against his as she ground her pelvis against his hard flesh. "Tell me you brought a condom."

"In my wallet. Let me get it."

He left her side for a moment, taking his heat with him while he searched his wallet for the protection they both needed.

"How long has that one been in there?"

"Quite a while actually," he said sliding the latex over his engorged cock.

"I wanted to taste you."

"Later. I need to be inside you."

She closed her eyes and sighed a happy sigh when he positioned his cock at her opening and slowly slid deep into her pussy.

"Fuck, you feel fantastic."

"Deeper, Joel. Please."

She pulled her legs up to her chest, opening herself for his deep thrust. He didn't disappoint as he slammed his pelvis against hers, pushing everything he had inside her much deeper than he'd been before. Each thrust pushed her across the bed until he grabbed her hips and held her still.

"Come for me, Mesa. Squeeze me until I explode. I wanna feel your heat."

With a small thought in her brain, she grabbed the pillow from the bed and put it over her face as she screamed his name at the top of her lungs.

Within seconds, he growled her name while he shot every bit of his cum into the end of the condom.

He laid his head on her chest as the air sawed in and out of his lungs in a deep pant.

"Was that makeup sex?" she asked with a giggle.

He chuckled a dry laugh before he peeked up at her through his gorgeous lashes. "I guess you could call it makeup sex. After all, we were having a pretty big fight." He kissed her quickly. "I'm sorry."

"Me too."

He slipped out of her and disposed of the condom in the small trashcan near the bathroom door. "I hope everyone in the dining room didn't hear us."

"I tried to be quiet but it's kind of hard with you."

He grinned a silly grin. "I'm glad I make you lose all control."

"Yes, you do cowboy." She frowned.

"What's the frown for?"

"What are we gonna do, Joel? This can't possibly work into anything beyond a few fun-filled days before I go back to California."

"Let's take it slow. Okay? I don't know what's goin' on here either, but I like you a lot, Mesa, and I don't like fighting with you. We have a good time together."

"All right. Slow. Got it."

"Would you show me what you've written today?"

"No!"

"Why not?"

She chewed her lip. There wasn't any way she could show Joel her new book since it paralleled what had happened to her on the ranch. "I never let anyone but my editor read my stuff until it's been published."

"But I want to read it."

"Not until it's done. I don't know what the ending is going to be yet and I don't want to spoil it until I get there. I only wrote about five thousand words today so the whole plot has a long way to go development-wise before it's done. I never know how they are going to turn out until I'm finished. And even then there's times when I change my mind about parts."

"All right, all right. I won't look then."

She crawled up on the bed to lay her head on the pillow. He took the spot next to her and gathered her into his arms. He kissed her hair while his hand did a slow crawl from her shoulder to her wrist.

"I love holding you like this."

"You just want me naked next to you."

His cock stirred, taking on a life of its own. "Well, yes. I love you naked any way I can get you."

"Typical man."

A knock sounded on the door. "Are you two okay in there?"

"Yeah, Ma. There's no blood. We're fine."

"Good. I'll see you in the morning."

"Night, Ma."

"Night, Nina." She snuggled down closer to his chest. "Kind of awkward, don't you think?"

"Nah. I think my mom was trying to get us together like this."

"Why? She knows I don't live here. It's not like this could possibly develop into a relationship."

"It can't?"

"No. I have my life in Los Angeles. You have your life here. We are two very different people, Joel."

"She's playing matchmaker again. She told me to stay away from you earlier."

Mesa laughed. "She told me the same thing this morning. I should avoid you today."

"Sneaky woman, my mother."

"Yep. She knew by telling us to stay away from each other, it would force a blowup and eventually we would have to talk. Thus, leading to this."

"Well, she might not have thought it through to this end, but she definitely had it right about staying away from each other. I can't."

She rubbed her face against his chest, loving the feel of the springy hair beneath her cheek. "Me either. You're like a drug. I can't get enough."

"I say we let it go where it may. If this is supposed to be something besides a short term thing, it will work itself out."

She pressed her lips together, thinking about the situation. Could she walk away after her week here was over without regrets? Probably not, but she had to. Her life in Los Angeles came first. She was a writer after all. A semi-famous author who had a full, rewarding life in the big city. She liked having stores around the corner. She enjoyed having the nightlife and clubs to visit if she so chose to, not that she was much of a nightlife person, but the option was there.

Here you would have the abundance of ranch life to jumpstart your muse. You would have the quiet, the horses, the cowboys, and the little bar in Bandera where you could dance the night away in the arms of one hot cowboy.

But what if things with Joel didn't work out? What if she gave up her life in Los Angeles, moved here to be with him, and they broke up after a time?

I could always move back to Los Angeles at any time.

"You aren't helping."

"Huh?" he asked sleepily when she glanced up at his face. His eyes were closed and his breathing had slowed into slumber. "Did you say something?"

"No. Go to sleep, big guy."

Soft snores reached her ears moments later as she snuggled back against his chest. There wouldn't be any use trying to make a decision like this on a whim. Like he said, let's take it slow and see where things go. If it's meant to be, it's meant to be. She should be able to make a decision by the time her week at the ranch went by.

Now, if she could just keep her heart from being the deciding factor in the whole thing, she might be able to make an intelligent decision.

Chapter Ten

Sunlight streamed through the window, dragging her from her dreams. Dreams of Joel danced behind her eyelids, keeping her from fully awakening to the birds chirping outside and the low bawl of cattle in the distance. She could get used to these sounds. The quiet country sounds instead of the blare of car horns, the chatter of people below her window, the bark of neighborhood dogs and the hustle of everyone in the city. No one slowed down to appreciate the things in life.

She reached to the side of the bed expecting to find Joel's warm body next to her only to find cold sheets. She sat up, pushing the hair from her eyes and looked around the room. His clothes were gone.

"Well duh, Mesa. He works on a cattle ranch. He has to be up with the chickens."

The clock on the table read seven-thirty. She jumped out of the bed, grabbed some clean clothes, and headed for the shower. Breakfast would be served in thirty minutes and she still had to be presentable. She wasn't sure why she cared so much since it was a cattle ranch. They lived with dirt and mud every day, so what difference did it make?

She lifted her arm and sniffed. "Okay. I do need a shower."

Several moments later, she stood beneath the warm spray of the water and drifted into a little daydream. Joel's lips on hers, firmly taking what he wanted. His hands, slick with soap, drifting down over her breasts and pinching her nipples between his fingers. The feel of his lips on the tight nubs, pulling and sucking them between his lips, drove her desire higher. Her hand drifted down between her thighs to touch her clit. A soft moan escaped on a sigh.

"Are you touching what's mine?"

Now her fantasy had a voice.

"I want you."

"Open your eyes."

She opened her eyes to find him standing at the bathroom door, leaning against the frame with a wicked grin on his lips.

The screech she released made him laugh. "What the hell? How did you get in here?"

"Master key."

"I thought you were working. I was trying to get cleaned up for breakfast."

"You looked like you were enjoying yourself a bit. Mind if I join you? I could use a shower, too."

"Somehow I don't think we'll be doing a lot of showering."

"I hope not. Watching you touch yourself was so fuckin' hot, I almost came in my jeans." He quickly stripped off his clothes and climbed into the shower with her. "Much better." He grabbed the soap and lathered up his hands until they were slick. "Now I can touch you like I wanted to this morning before I left your bed."

"Why didn't you?" she asked, whispering along his throat. "I would have loved to wake up like that."

He ran his hands over her breasts. "Because I didn't want to wake you. You were sleeping so peacefully with a beautiful smile on your lips."

"I was dreaming of you like this."

He laughed as he pinched her nipples, drawing them to little points of pleasure. "In the shower? I thought that dream came when you were touching yourself."

"Well yes, but I dreamt of you just the same, touching me, loving me. I can't get enough."

He slanted his mouth over hers, driving his tongue between her lips in the erotic dance only two lovers know. His hands skimmed down her abdomen and around to her hips to draw her closer to his body. His rock-hard erection pressed into her stomach. "Do you want me?" she asked, pulling away from his kiss to lick his throat.

"Oh, hell yeah. I snuck away from my chores to have you."

"So romantic, you are." She released a throaty laugh as she nipped at his skin. She wanted to bite him, eat him up until he couldn't escape her feast on his flesh.

One of his hands slid around to the front of her body to dive between her thighs. "God, you're wet."

"I'm in the shower," she said with a laugh before it turned to a moan the minute he thrust two fingers inside her pussy. "Okay, that's not because of the shower."

"Let me grab a condom."

She glanced into his eyes. "I don't want a barrier between us."

"What are you saying, Mesa?"

"I'm clean and I'm on birth control. Are you?"

"Clean, yes."

"Then fuck me, Joel."

He put both hands under her buttocks. "Wrap your legs around me."

"You can't li—"

"I wrestle cows for a livin', darlin'. I can handle a little thing like you."

He lifted her in his arms and she wrapped both legs around his waist. With her back against the cold tile, he slid home, filling her to the brim with his hard flesh. Her satisfied moan echoed off the tile enclosure.

"God, you feel good, baby."

"Move, Joel. I need you."

He rocked his hips back and forth, sliding his scalding length deep inside her. His groan matched hers. Ecstasy fogged her brain. Water beat down upon them in a cascade, pounding in a solid stream between them as he continued to rock his hips.

"Damn, I'm not gonna last like this. The sensation is killing me."

"Make me come."

He shifted his stance. The slide of his cock hit her G spot in exactly the right place to shoot her desire to explosive. She exploded on a cry, his name a mantra from her lips. Stars burst behind her eyelids, blinding her to anything but the feeling of him deep inside her.

His own climax echoed hers until she felt the stickiness of their mingled cum sliding down her leg.

She rested her head on his chest, dragging air into her starved lungs until her head cleared and she could think straight again.

"I like it much better without the barrier between us."

"Me too, but I didn't want to push."

The breakfast bell clanged, startling them both. He pulled out of her and grabbed the soap to finish washing her. "We need to hurry or we're gonna miss breakfast."

"We can always hit the diner in town."

"Don't you have work to do?"

"Yeah, but I'll already be in hot water for skipping out this morning."

"I don't want you to be in trouble."

"It's okay. Josh covered for me."

"He knew you were coming up here to seduce me?"

"I didn't tell him if that's what you mean. I think he might have assumed so from the silly grin on my face." He washed himself, and then waited for her.

She quickly washed her hair and rinsed in the warm water that seemed to be turning colder by the second. "I think we're about to run out of hot water."

"Yeah, I think so too. Hurry."

"I am." Within minutes, she'd washed every bit of soap off and grabbed one of the fluffy, white towels hanging on the wall to dry herself with as Joel rinsed.

He shut the water off then pulled the other towel down.

"What time did you wake up this morning?" she asked, heading back into the bedroom with the pile of her clean clothes.

"I'm always up when the sun comes up. We have to feed and water the animals before we take them out for the day."

"I know the bed was already cold by the time I woke."

"Yeah, I'd already been up for a couple of hours by then."

"Wow."

"Do you want to go to town?"

"Sure."

They dressed in a rush in between kissing and touching. His lips found her throat as he nibbled from her earlobe to her collarbone. "If you don't stop, we'll never get out of here. Food calls," she said in between moans of ecstasy and trying to button his shirt.

"Maybe I want something else to eat."

Her pussy creamed at the thought, soaking her panties. She loved when he ate her out. "Later, cowboy. My stomach needs sustenance."

"Party pooper," he replied, pressing his forehead against hers. "Promise?"

"Oh yeah."

"Okay, let's get food then." He stepped into his boots as she tied her tennis shoes. "Did you bring boots?"

"I hadn't planned on being on a ranch. I really should go buy some, I guess."

"Yes, you should, especially if you plan on ridin' with me."

"Riding you?"

"With me, Mesa, but I'll take the other, too."

"I bet you would, cowboy."

About fifteen minutes later, they pulled up to the front of a quaint little diner situated near the light in the middle of Bandera.

"Does everyone come here?"

"A lot of the older crowd comes for coffee early and so do many of the wranglers. They shoot the shit during the morning before they head out for the day's work."

"This place sounds so fun." She took out the pen and paper she always kept in her purse to jot down some notes on the diner. A waitress showed them to a booth near the window. Joel took one side and she took the other. She set the book aside to glance at the menu. A ham and cheese omelet sounded good to her.

"What are you havin'?"

"Omelet. You?"

"Bacon and eggs."

The waitress appeared at their table, barely glancing at Mesa, but focusing entirely on Joel. "Hey, Joel."

"Hey, Marie. Coffee, Mesa?"

"Yes please."

He looked up at the waitress and said, "Two coffees. I'll have bacon and eggs over medium with hash browns and my lady friend will have?"

"Ham and cheese omelet."

"Got that?"

"Yeah," she said, simpering over him and batting her eyes. "Are you busy tonight?"

"Yes, I am actually."

"What about tomorrow night?"

"Sorry, Marie. I'm not interested in dating you. We've already had this discussion before. You're a sweet girl, but you aren't my type."

"And she is? Look at her!"

"What's between me and Mesa is none of your business. I'll thank you to remember that and please call us another waitress."

"But I…"

"Ann?"

"Yeah, Joel?" an older woman called from behind the counter.

"Can you come here and take our order please."

"Be right there." She grabbed a coffee pot and two cups before she headed over toward their table. "I got this, Marie."

Marie huffed off toward the kitchen, glancing behind her several times.

"Sorry about her, Joel. You know she's had the hots for you for a long time. She just doesn't know when to quit."

"It's fine. I just didn't want to subject my friend here to her."

Ann poured them two cups of coffee, smiling at Mesa and whole time. "You ain't from around here."

"No, I'm staying at the ranch for a few days."

"Ann Quimby, this is Mesa Arraguso. She's from L.A."

"Nice to meet you, Ann," Mesa replied, taking her hand in a firm shake.

"You too, Mesa. I ain't sure how you corralled this youngin', but hang on tight. You're in for the ride of your life, honey."

Mesa blushed to the roots of her hair. Was it so obvious they were sleeping together that the whole town could tell by looking at them? "Thanks for the advice."

"No problem, darlin'. What are you two eatin'?"

Joel repeated the order to Ann then she took off toward the kitchen to get their order up. Mesa bit her lip and sipped her coffee. Joel watched her over the rim of his cup, his eyebrow raised over his left eye. "What?"

"You're blushin'."

"I didn't think it was so obvious we're lovers, but apparently it is."

"Are you ashamed, because I'm not."

"No. I really didn't think it was written on my forehead though." She tapped the spot between her brows. "You know. Joel's slut."

"You aren't a slut, Mesa, for God's sake. There's a big difference between someone who goes around sleeping with everyone and anyone and someone who hooks up with one person for a short term fling."

"Did you just hear yourself? It means the same thing, Joel."

"No, it doesn't." He lowered his voice. "Sluts sleep with everyone or anyone. You are only sleepin' with me. Of course, we aren't doin' much sleepin'."

"Shush. I don't want everyone hearing you."

"It's none of their business what we do, Mesa."

"I still don't need everyone hearing you talk about our sex life."

"What does it matter? After you leave, you won't ever see them again."

"What if I come back?"

"Are you?"

"Am I what?"

"Coming back after you leave."

"I don't know, Joel. It all depends on what happens between us. I mean, maybe we could just have a fling every year around the same time." She sipped her coffee before setting the cup back down. "Isn't there a movie with the same storyline? I know." She snapped her fingers. "It's called Same Time Next Year. We could do that."

He drank a little of his coffee. "I don't want to think about when you're goin' home."

"I don't either, but it's reality. I have a life back in Los Angeles. Your life is here."

"You're becoming a very important part of my life, Mesa."

"Here you go, folks. Omelet for the lady. Bacon and eggs for you, Joel. More coffee?"

"No, I think we're good, Ann. Thank you."

They ate in silence while the thoughts of going home soured her stomach. She didn't want to go back to Los Angeles. She didn't care about her life there anymore, but Joel didn't want to talk about her leaving either.

After they finished their breakfast and quietly sipped their coffee, Joel asked, "Are you finished? We can hit the small western wear store for a pair of boots before we go back to the ranch."

"Yes, I'm done."

She grabbed her wallet to pay for her breakfast, but he beat her to the tab, thrusting twenty dollars into Ann's hands as she brought the bill. "Keep the change."

"Thanks, doll. See you around?"

"Of course, darlin'. You know I can't stay away from you."

He kissed her on the cheek and jealousy rushed through Mesa. *What the hell? She's old enough to be his mother.*

"Tell my sister hello for me when you get back to the ranch."

"I will. Ma needs to come in here once in a while to get away from the house. She spends too much time on the books."

Her sister? Nina is Ann's sister? Well that explains the familiarity of Joel with Ann. She's his aunt!

"Are reservations up this year?"

"Yeah, business is doin' good. Now, if the damned housin' development people would back the hell off and quit buyin' up the properties, we'd be fine."

"Are they buyin' up more?"

"Yeah. One of our neighbors sold out."

"Y'all have enough land to keep them from bein' too close to you."

"True, but it cuts down on the range land overall, which makes it difficult for the wildlife."

"True, baby doll." She patted his cheek before she hugged him. "Kiss your mama."

"Sure. Love you."

"Love you too, honey. Take care of that girl. She's good for you, Joel."

Color spread across his cheeks as he blushed a deep red. "I will."

The warmth of his hand at the small of her back made her feel cared for. She wasn't sure why having him show his possession of her on such a visceral level brought her spirits up, even when it wasn't what it seemed.

Next they hit the western store for boots. He helped her pick out a nice part of Ariat boots with soft rawhide. The pair hugged her feet, molding to the shape of her foot so well, she felt like she was walking in slippers. "These are fabulous, Joel. Thank you for helping me pick them out."

"You're welcome, darlin'. I have a pair similar in my closet I wear out dancing because they are so comfortable."

"Do you go to the club a lot?"

"I wouldn't say a lot. I don't go every weekend or anything."

"What else do you like to do?"

"Huntin', fishin', four-wheelin', muddin'. You know, outdoorsy things."

"What's muddin'?"

"You've never been muddin'?"

She laughed and punched his arm. "If I had, I wouldn't have asked you what it is, now would I?"

"Well hell, darlin'. We'll get the boys together after work this evenin' and show you what a good time muddin' is! We usually do it on the weekend when we don't have so much work, but it's fun in the dark, too. We get the big ass lights on the back of the truck, turn them on and have a great time."

"So what is it?"

"We get our trucks out in the big mud bog down near the fishin' hole and race around in it. It's a blast! You get mud in places you never thought you'd see mud."

"Sounds like fun."

"Let's head back to the ranch. I need to do a little work today if we are gonna get everyone to cut out early tonight. Mom and Dad will probably go, too. Hell, they might even invite all the guests. We sometimes get people settin' up their lawn chairs out there just to watch. Some of the guys from town come out too if they know we are doin' it, just to join in." Joel helped her into his truck before he went around to the driver's side. "This is gonna be fun. We haven't been muddin' in several weeks. It's been too busy at the ranch."

"Are you sure it'll be okay?"

"It'll be great. It's been kind of slow at the ranch this week so Mom and Dad shouldn't have a problem with it."

He started the truck and backed out of the spot at the western wear store.

Several minutes later, he punched the code into the gate at the front of the ranch. "Why do you lock the gate?"

"Mostly to keep unwanted visitors out. We have a pool and some of the local kids want to come by and swim. We don't have a lifeguard, so for liability issues, we keep the place locked. It also keeps out the people wandering around looking for ranches to check out. We've had people poach our cattle before."

"Wow, really?"

"Yeah. We have the longhorns who roam the ranch, but we also have the beef cattle we use to sell for meat."

They pulled up in the front of the main lodge as Nina stepped outside. She waved and started for the truck. "I'm going to the barn," he said once they stood in front of it.

"Chicken."

"Yep. I don't want another lecture from my mother about our love life." He reached over and kissed her. "I'll see you after while. I'll get the guys set up for muddin' later. You just wear somethin' you won't mind gettin' all dirty in."

"Yes, Sir."

His left eyebrow rose. "I like when you say that. We'll work on it more later." He kissed her again just as Nina reached the truck. "Later, Mom."

"Where are you goin'?"

"To work."

"You haven't done anything all morning, young man. What's makin' you start now?"

He grinned and started to whistle as he made his way toward the barn without answering her.

"Where'd you two go? I didn't see you at breakfast."

"We went to the diner in town since we were late getting up."

Nina grinned. "I'm glad you two are gettin' along much better."

"Not that you had anything to do with us not talking to each other yesterday and then getting into a big fight so we would make up."

"Me?"

"Playing matchmaker, Nina?"

"I just want my son to be happy. You make him happy." She shrugged. "I haven't seen him in such a good mood in a long time."

"We've come to a mutual agreement."

"Oh?"

"Yes. We aren't going to talk about anything past this week."

"What happens after this week?"

"We don't know at this point. We're playing it by ear, so to speak."

Nina tilted her head, giving Mesa a look like her mother would. "What do you want to happen?"

"I have a life in Los Angeles, Nina. Joel is a great guy and we get along fine, but I don't think there is anything beyond this week for us."

"I'm sorry to hear you say that, Mesa. I think you two are fabulous together, but I understand where you are coming from. Moving all the way here would be a huge mistake on your part. I mean what happens if things don't work out between you and Joel?"

"I've been telling myself the same thing for the last couple of days. I'm glad you understand."

"I really do, but let me tell you a story."

"Okay." Mesa took a seat on the picnic bench as Nina sat across from her.

"I wasn't born and raised here."

"But you're Native American."

"Yes, I am, but Texas is not where I came from. I met the boys' father when I traveled with my own father to Washington on a business trip. He was high counsel in our tribe. The trip was to try to talk the government into giving us more money for schools and medicine. We didn't have access to a clinic for the young girls to go for birth control and my father wanted me to talk to them as a teenager on the verge of womanhood with all the sexual urges of a budding young lady."

"Wow."

"Yep."

"Did you meet Mr. Young there?"

"No. He worked for the government agency and was sent to the area to do a report on our needs after my father gave them his plea. He was a suit and a half when he walked into our home to talk to my father. I'd never seen such a man before except for those in Washington. The only people I'd seen were those of our hometown in New Mexico."

"You two were so drawn to each other, he moved out here, bought the ranch, and moved you to it to raise your family."

Nina laughed. "Oh, if only it were so romantic. No. I hated him on sight. He was arrogant and self-righteous. But he kept coming back. We saw him several times over a two-year period. I came to realize he wanted to do what was best for us no matter what the government said we needed. He helped us in ways no one knew. I turned eighteen the last summer he came. We got to talking one day out by my parents barn. He reached over and kissed me. Shocked me somethin' fierce. I didn't know what to make of it. You see, I'd never been kissed before. I held onto my virginity like a sacred vow to the gods and I wasn't going to give it up to just anyone. James swept me off my feet, but then he didn't come back. I didn't see him again for five years. He went back to Washington and left me in New Mexico without a word. He never wrote, never called, nothing."

"I'm sorry."

"It was for the best. I wasn't ready to be anything but a young girl when he was there during that summer, but when he returned I knew what I wanted. I wanted him and I wasn't going to take no for an answer. I knew he liked me or he wouldn't have kissed me." She laughed. "I made him work for it though. No, I wasn't easy to catch when he returned the bit older man. You see, he's ten years my senior so at eighteen, I wasn't old enough for him, but at twenty five, I knew what I wanted." Nina took Mesa's hand in hers. "All I'm saying is if you want Joel, don't let him go. He might not be there when you're ready for him." Nina patted her hand and climbed to her feet. "I have a feeling there is more between you than either of you is willing to admit. Just don't let it be too late. I got lucky."

Nina moved off toward the house leaving Mesa to think things through on her own. Thinking wasn't part of the plan though. Thinking meant she had to feel and she wasn't sure she wanted to let her heart do the talking.

Chapter Eleven

The roar of the trucks sent tingles down her arms as they sat on the edge of the mud pit waiting for the signal. Joel sat in the driver's seat with her buckled into the passenger seat. Her heart raced in excitement. She had her hair pulled back in a ponytail and wondered if she really would get as muddy as Joel suggested. She kind of hoped so. This would be one hell of an experience to add to the authenticity of her cowboy romances.

"Ready?" he asked, flashing her a wide grin. His eyes sparkled like blue topaz in the dim light of the truck cab.

She could tell he was totally in his element here amongst his brothers and friends with their beer, trucks, mud to their elbows, and country music turned up so loud she could hardly understand the words.

"Yeah." She gripped the *oh shit* handle so tight, her knuckles turned white.

The girl holding the flags on the other side of the pit threw her arms ups and they were off. Mud sprayed the sides of the trucks practically obliterating the view out the windows. They slipped and slid around in circles. Mesa laughed as Joel kept the truck upright. She never had so much fun in her life.

After they had their turn at the pit, they drank beer, roasted hot dogs and marshmallows over the open bonfire, told stories, and laughed until their stomachs hurt. Some of the trucks from town even came out when they heard the Young family was havin' a muddin' party.

Mesa had mud in her pants from when Joel tossed her in before diving in after her. Not to mention the muck in her hair, down her shirt and everywhere in between but she hated to see it end.

The mud had begun to dry on her skin, pulling it tight. She couldn't wait to get back to her room and into a nice, warm shower. Her eyes began to droop as she snuggled up into the curve of Joel's arms. He'd sat on the ground with his back against a rock, drawing her into the cocoon of his embrace.

"Ready for bed?"

"Hmm. Yeah, if you're in it."

"I hoped to be. I need a shower first though."

"Me too."

"How about we head back to my place, shower, make love, and sleep until noon tomorrow?"

"Yeah, right. You'll be up with the chickens."

"True, but one can dream, right? I wanna hold you tonight."

"I need to stop by my room and get clean clothes then."

"Okay." He stood up, drawing her up with him. "We're headin' back to the house. See y'all in the mornin'."

The good-natured ribbing brought a smile to her face. Not like anyone in the group knew for sure, but they had an idea what would happen when they made it to a bed.

"You got condoms, brother? I think you're gonna need a few."

"Don't worry about me, Jeremiah. I'm prepared. Trust me."

The group laughed as she blushed to the roots of her hair. Good thing they couldn't see her face in the dark.

"We're going to get the interior of your truck dirty."

"It washes. I got leather interior for a reason. This is what we do around the Hill Country."

"Tonight blew my mind, Joel. You guys were great. I can see why you love it here so much."

"I do. It's where I was born and raised. I can see bringing up my kids here."

"You want kids?"

"Someday, yeah. A couple. Nothing like my parents. Wow. I couldn't handle nine boys, I don't think. I don't know how they did it."

"I can't imagine it either. I mean I have a couple of siblings, but nine..."

They pulled up in front of the house. "I'll just be a minute if you want to wait here."

"I'll walk with you. I've been walking this ground my whole life. I know every pot hole, rock, and nook in this yard, but there are still dangers of walking out here at night and I have a flashlight on my key ring for just this purpose."

"Always prepared, huh?"

"I try to be, but you've thrown me for a loop more times than I can count."

"Me?"

"Yes, ma'am. I wish I knew what to do with you."

"Just love me."

He tripped over a rock and she laughed.

"So much for knowin' every rock."

He grinned as he swatted her butt.

She took off at a run up the steps of the house and through the doorway. They laughed as he chased her up the stairs to her door. With a hand on either side of her head, he trapped her against the door.

"Now you're mine."

Her lips parted on a sigh. "I've been yours from the moment I rode behind you on your horse."

"Are you, because I need to know."

"Yes."

He bent his head to take her lips in a soul-searing kiss meant to curl her toes, which it did. She tangled her fingers in the hair at the nape of his neck. His tongue tangled with hers, spreading warmth from her mouth to every part of her body. Her belly clenched in need. She needed this man with every breath in her body.

When he lifted his head, his eyes were darker blue and burning with lust. "We can shower here."

"Let me get the door."

"I want you, Mesa," he whispered against her ear when she turned around to unlock the door. Shivers rolled down her back as goose bumps flittered across her arms.

They stumbled through the doorway.

"What the hell?" they said in unison.

Every drawer on all the furniture was open although nothing seemed disturbed in the drawers. She looked around the room, but nothing was missing.

"It had to be the ghosts."

"Ghosts?"

"Yeah, they've been bugging me since I got here. Knocking on my door when there is no one there, voices, arguing, the cowboy who disappeared."

"Oh."

"Yeah, oh. You know about them, right?"

"Yes. They don't usually bug people or do this kind of stuff though. They get a little noisy sometimes, but I've never had them open drawers like this."

"Well, it doesn't matter. You're here. He won't bug me tonight."

"He?"

"Yeah, the cowboy or the guy who argues with the women next door. I think it's her knocking on my door sometimes, but I'm not sure. There isn't anyone there when I answer."

"You're okay with all this?"

She shrugged as she removed his cowboy hat and threw it on the bed. "I have to be, Joel. They are part of this house. If they leave me alone, I'm fine with sharing their space."

"You're an amazing woman, Mesa."

"Thank you, now get naked."

"Yes, ma'am." He grinned, unzipping and stepping out of his jeans after he pushed them to the floor.

His full length made her mouth water to taste, but she burst out laughing.

* * * *

"What the hell is so funny?" he asked indignation rushing through him while he watched Mesa double over in a fit of giggles.

"You...mud...on...your..."

He smiled when he looked down and saw mud caked on his cock. Well, it wasn't a good muddin' trip if there wasn't mud everywhere. "Shower now, woman."

She continued to laugh as she removed her clothes and left them in a pile on the wood floor so they wouldn't get the carpet dirty with the mud. Too late. It seemed to be everywhere.

He followed her into the bathroom and began rubbing his hard cock between her butt cheeks while she adjusted the temperature on the shower until the water seemed warm enough. "Easy, big boy."

"Hell no. I'm fuckin' you in the shower against the tile wall."

"Oh yeah?"

"Yep."

"Let's get the mud and crud out of my hair before we do the nasty."

"The nasty, huh?"

"Of course. Haven't you heard the term before?"

He laughed. "Not put like that, I haven't." Her butt looked delectable when she turned around to wash her face. He squeezed a cheek as a moan escaped his mouth. What he wouldn't give to bury his cock in between those hot little cheeks. *Would she let him eventually? Interesting thought.*

After she spun around to wash her hair, he grabbed the soap to lather up her breasts. *Man, she has pretty tits, too.* "I love your tits."

"Breasts, Joel," she said rising her hair while he enjoyed himself with the soap. "Women don't like them called tits. It's vulgar."

"What about this?" he asked, sliding his hand down between her legs.

"Pussy is fine by me, but I don't like cunt."

"Fine. I want your pussy squeezing me."

"I want that too."

"Are you wet for me?"

"Fuck yes." She moaned, tossing her head back as he worked her pussy with his fingers.

Her hard little clit poked out for his touch. He wanted to eat her until she creamed all over his face, but for now, he was going to fuck her against the wall.

He twirled her around so he could wash himself real quick. He wanted to get down to the good stuff in short order. She laughed when he washed his hair and body in record time.

"Anxious are we?"

"Horny would be a better word for it," he said, rinsing the last of the soap from his chest. He leaned down and kissed her as he wrapped her in his arms. *God, I love kissing her, touching her...loving her. Where the hell did that thought come from? I don't love her. I can't. She's leaving in a couple of days.*

"What's wrong?" she asked when he cut the kiss short.

Joel shook his head and leaned back down to kiss her again as he whispered, "Nothin'." He slid his tongue past her lips to tangle with hers. With his fingers, he pinched her nipples into hard little points like he knew she enjoyed. His little city girl liked a little pain with her sex. A soft moan escaped her mouth around their kiss. He lifted her with both hands on her butt cheeks until she wrapped her legs around his hips and pushed her against the wall of the shower. "Give me everythin', darlin'."

"You have everything, Joel."

I want your heart.

He nudged his cock against her opening and slowly slid as deep as he could possibly get. "Aw, fuck."

"Do it. Fuck me."

He braced his feet wide apart so they didn't slip in the shower and fucked her until she screamed his name on a prayer.

His balls drew up against his groin and he knew he wouldn't last much longer. She needed to come again before he let go.

"Play with your clit."

"What?" she asked in a panting whisper.

"Play with your clit. Make yourself come again."

"But…"

"Do it now."

She snaked her hand down between their joined bodies until she reached her clit. With her head back against the shower stall, she completely lost herself in the pleasure she built with her fingers while he slowly guided his cock in and out. *God, she's beautiful.* "Come for me, darlin'."

A high scream echoed off the stall doors when she climaxed the second time, drawing his own from deep inside his body to explode inside her with gushing spurts. His legs shook as he tried desperately to draw air into his starving lungs.

"Oh my God."

"Yeah, you can say that again." He slowly let her legs down and helped her stand on her own two feet. "You're fabulous."

"You are pretty good yourself."

They quickly washed the cum from their bodies before they climbed out and dried off. "Do you want to stay here instead of going to your place?"

"I can make you scream more at my place. No neighbors."

"True. I'm not quite done with you yet, cowboy."

"Good. I ain't nearly done with you yet, city girl."

They got dressed and then snuck down the stairs, listening for any noise from the family to know whether they'd come back from the muddin' party. She giggled like a child as they sprinted toward the door on tiptoes, trying to be quiet even though he didn't think anyone had come home yet.

He pulled the door open to come face to face with Jeff.

"Where the hell are you goin'?"

"Back to my place. Later, brother."

Jeff just shook his head as they went around him laughing as they took off running hand in hand toward his truck.

"We can't take this, Joel. It's full of mud on the seats."

"Let's take your car then."

"Let's just stay here."

"Fine by me, babe. I just didn't think you wanted everyone in the house to know how loud you get when you come."

"Let's take my car." She pulled the keys from her purse and unlocked her car that sat two spots down from his truck.

It only took a few minutes for them to reach his cabin, get inside and strip down to skin. He loved having her close. *There's that word again. I am not in love with Mesa.*

"What's wrong?"

"Nothin', why?"

"You're frowning as you look at me. It's kind of hard on the ego, you know."

"Sorry. I just had a thought."

"What?"

"It's nothin', really. I'm sad you're leavin' in a couple of days."

"Yeah. I know."

"Let's not think about it right now. Okay? I wanna love you all night long."

"An all-nighter, huh?"

"Oh yeah." He drew her down in front of the fireplace.

"Too bad it's too warm for a fire. I've always wanted to make love in front of a fire."

He held up one finger. "Wait right there." He walked to the thermostat and cranked up the air conditioning. "Now, it'll get cold in here so we can have a fire." The fireplace was gas logs so he just hit the switch and ignited the thing. "How's that?" he asked, snuggling down on the rug and pulling her into the crook of his arm. Nothing like a willing female to appreciate in front of a roaring fire.

"Perfect. Thank you. You don't know how much this means to me."

"Me too. I love the way the firelight bounces color off your skin."

"My pale skin, you mean."

"No." He kissed her shoulder and run his tongue along the curve until he reached her neck. "You have fabulous skin. All soft beneath my tongue. I love your taste."

"I didn't realize I had a taste."

"You do. Sweet with a little tang. It's addicting."

"Is it?"

"Yep."

She turned around in his arms until she rose up on her knees between his legs. "I like your taste, too." Her tongue danced along his jaw until she reached his ear. "I could fall in love with you so easily."

He pushed her back and looked into her eyes. Sincerity and insecurity shone bright in her gaze. Did she really mean what she said? Was she in love with him? What about his feelings for her? Did he feel love for this enigma of a woman who'd turned his life upside down since he found her on the side of the road?

"Don't freak, Joel. I just meant if we had more time."

He exhaled on a rush.

"Make love to me."

He pushed her back on the rug and kissed her from the tip of her nose, over her shoulder, across her breasts, down her abdomen, settling between her legs. "I'm gonna eat you until you cream for me."

She moaned softly and closed her eyes.

Her pussy glistened with her juices in the firelight as he looked at all the pink flesh. She wasn't a waxer, but she obviously kept it well clipped. No stray hairs anywhere. Funny he hadn't really noticed before.

"What are you doing?"

"Lookin' my fill. You are so gorgeous, you take my breath away."

"It's bit disconcerting to have a man between your legs just so he can look."

"We like to look." He licked from pussy to clit in one long stroke.

Her head fell back on the carpeted floor as she growled deep in her throat.

He loved the way she tasted, too. He loved everything about her. *God, I'm so screwed.*

Not willing to give into the feelings surging through him at the moment, he loved her until she came twice by his tongue and his fingers. He moved up between her thighs. With one skillful snap of his hips, he buried his cock so deep inside her, he knew he'd come home.

* * * *

Two days later Mesa stood at the side of her car as Joel loaded her suitcases. Nina hugged her with tears in her eyes. "You know you can come back anytime, honey. You'll always be welcome."

"Thanks, Nina, but I'm not sure I can."

"He loves you, you know."

"No, I don't think so."

"He's just bein' stubborn. He's a man after all."

"I know, but I don't think things would work out between us even if I were here permanently. We're too different."

"Wait and see."

"Everythin' is in the trunk, Mesa."

"Thanks, Joel."

"I'll leave you two to your goodbyes. You take care, honey. Call and let us know you got home all right. I'll worry until you do."

Nina hugged her again. "Thank you for everything," she whispered in the older woman's ear.

"You're welcome."

Joel stood off to the side with his hands in his pockets until his mother walked back to the house. "Come 'ere."

Tears spilled down her cheeks as she hugged him close to her heart. She loved him. She knew she did, but she couldn't give up her life in Los Angeles to move to a small town in Texas and she couldn't ask him to leave the only life he knew to do what? He would be so out of place in Los Angeles, it would be comical.

He moved back and wiped the tears from her cheeks. "Don't cry, darlin'."

"I'm gonna miss you."

"I'm gonna miss you too." He glanced at his watch. "You better get goin' or you'll miss your flight."

She closed her eyes and sniffed, holding back the tears without success. "Bye, Joel."

"Bye, darlin'."

Chapter Twelve

"You're being an asshole, Joel. Go fuckin' get laid or something!" Jonathan yelled as the two of them stood toe-to-toe in the barn.

He knew his brother was right. He'd been a total dick the last few weeks, but he didn't know what to do to fix it. "Fuck you."

"Go find some chick to fuck and get it over with. Mesa left. You didn't stop her. It's your own damn fault you let her get away and now you're miserable. You're totally in love with her."

"I'm not in love with her, damn it!"

"The hell you aren't. Look at yourself. You barely eat, you aren't sleepin', and I bet you haven't been able to fuck another woman since she left."

"What difference does that make?"

"You couldn't could you? You tried and you couldn't get it up."

"Get the hell away from me before I kick your ass."

"Try it!" Jonathan put up his fists and backed up. "I'm waiting."

"You aren't worth the bruise on my knuckles." He stomped off, heading for the peace and quiet of the main lodge. Guests were few this week, so he should be able to sulk in private. He hoped.

A few moments later, he stood by the window of the main lodge looking out over the front of the house. He hadn't talked to Mesa in a month, not since she walked out of his life. Miserable would describe his state of mind since she left. His life had come down to this, up at dawn, ride the fences, help his brother break horses, feed the animals, and mope the evening away with a bottle of beer and his television. He couldn't eat, couldn't sleep and certainly couldn't even think about being with another woman. He'd tried that. The weekend after she left, he'd gotten drunk at the bar in town, took someone home and then couldn't preform. The woman had left pissed.

"Son, why don't you call her?"

"Because I can't, Ma. She doesn't love me."

"I think you're wrong."

"Why wouldn't she say it then?" he asked, turning to face her.

"She's just as stubborn as you are." Nina jammed her hands on her hips to take up her I'm-the-mother-so-listen-to-what-I'm-telling-you look. "Did you tell her you love her?"

"No."

"Then why would she say it first? Why do you think it's up to her to tell you, but you couldn't tell her?"

"I'm not in love with her, Ma."

"You really believe that, son? You've been miserable since she left. I've seen the way you mope around here like someone killed your dog. Give it up. I don't know if you think to convince me or yourself with that statement, but it won't work on me." She hugged him and stepped back. "You love her, Joel. It's written all over your face. You were happy when she was here. Go after her. Convince her you love her and bring her back home where she belongs. If you don't, you'll regret it for the rest of your life." She placed her hand on his cheek. "I love you, son, but you're drivin' us all nuts with this."

* * * *

Four weeks. It had been four damned weeks since she left Bandera and Joel. Mesa buried her faced in the pillow on her couch. She hadn't been able to eat, couldn't sleep, didn't want to do anything but dream of Joel where he visited every night. She was miserable. "This is fuckin' crazy!"

Her phone rang, but she didn't feel like answering it. Every time it rang the one person she wanted to talk to wasn't there. She'd made sure he had her phone number when she left, but so far, he hadn't used it. Obviously, he'd moved on without her. She needed to do the same. She just couldn't seem to breathe without thinking about him.

Her answering machine picked up and she heard the voice of her agent. "Mesa, darling. I need to talk to you about this book you sent me. Please pick up."

"All right, Mesa. I hate to say this, honey, but we can't publish this. We write romance. This doesn't have a happily ever after, honey. The heroine is miserable and we can't sell this to anyone. You are a talented woman beyond words, but this won't sell. You need to rewrite the ending. I'll call you this afternoon."

"I wish I fucking could!" she screamed at the answering machine, bursting into tears. "God, I wish it had a happy ending. I want my happy ending."

"Never mind. I'm at your door. We need to talk now."

The phone clicked indicating the woman had hung up just as the doorbell rang.

"Just fucking great." She buried her head in the pillow. "Maybe if I don't answer it, she'll leave."

"I know you're in there, Mesa. Your car is in the driveway. Open the door, honey."

Mesa sighed and climbed to her feet. She was just going to have to get this meeting over with so she could wallow in peace. "I'm coming!" she yelled as the doorbell rang again. "What do you want, Madeline?"

"You look like shit, darling. What the hell happened to you?"

"Nothing."

"Oh, something definitely. I've never seen you like this," Madeline said, shoving past her to enter her hallway. "Like I said on the phone, we can't sell this piece with this ending, Mesa. It won't do."

"I'm sorry, but it is what it is."

"You need to rewrite it. The hero and heroine have to come together somehow. Make him show up on her doorstep begging for her forgiveness and confessing his love. It's romantic. It's fun. It's what it needs."

Mesa closed her eyes as she exhaled a deep sigh. "I just can't right now, Madeline. Maybe in a few weeks I'll get over this melancholy me and be able to give them their happy ending."

"Honey, what happened in Texas?"

"Nothing."

"You look like someone died, darling."

"No. No one died. I'll get over it. I'll be back on track in no time. You'll see."

"A man?"

Her eyes widened. Surely Madeline couldn't tell she had a man on the brain, could she?

"I'm fine really. Thanks for stopping by." She pushed Madeline toward the door. "I'll call you next week. We can do lunch."

"All right. If you're sure."

"I'm sure. Thank you for being worried about me."

"Call me if you need anything. All right?"

"I will." She shut the door behind her agent and pressed her back against the wood panel. She really needed to get over Joel, now. "Enough. I can't keep doing this." She swiped at the tears rolling down her cheeks. "He obviously didn't love me. It was nothing more than a quick fling like he said from the beginning. I should never have let my heart get involved. Big mistake from the get go."

The doorbell rang, echoing the sound throughout her apartment until she wanted to scream. *Bong. Bong.* Whoever was out there wasn't going away until she answered the damn door.

"What?" she yelled as she opened the door to find a deliveryman.

"Ms. Arraguso?"

"Yes?"

He handed her the clipboard. "Sign here."

She signed her name and he handed her a single red rose. "That's it?"

"Yes, ma'am."

He walked away while she looked at the flower. *How weird.* Maybe it's from a fan. She closed the door and walked into her kitchen to set the beautiful blood red bud down. She needed a drink. Something strong. Lots of alcohol to drown her breaking heart in.

She poured whiskey straight from the bottle into a glass and then looked at the flower again. Something odd caught her attention, and she frowned as peered closer at the flower. "What the hell? There's writing on the petals."

She slowly peeled the silky layers back.

I can't eat.

I can't sleep.

I miss you.

I'm miserable without you.

The last one said…*I love you.*

A soft knock sounded on the front door as she stood there in shocked silence. Not even aware of what she was doing, she moved to the door and opened it to find Joel standing there in all his cowboy glory with eleven more blood red roses clutched in his hands. She let her gaze roam over him from the top of his black Stetson to the tips of the dirty cowboy boots. He looked good enough to eat.

"Do the tears mean you missed me, too?" he asked, his blue eyes hopeful.

"God, did I miss you!" She threw her arms around his neck and kissed him with all the pent up passion and love she held in her heart for this crazy man. "I love you. I love you. I love you." She punctuated each phrase with a kiss.

She heard the rest of the bouquet crunch to the carpet as he pulled her arms from around his neck and dropped to one knee. "Mesa, baby. Will you marry me?"

Mesa covered her mouth as more tears streamed down her cheeks. "Yes. I'll marry you. When? Where? Right now? Let's go to Vegas. We can be married today. It's only a four hour drive."

"Slow down, baby. I'd marry you today, but my family would kill me."

She stuck out her lip in a small pout, hoping he would give in. They could be married before the end of the day.

"I love you, Mesa."

"I love you too, Joel."

"We have to wait."

"Why?"

"Because, I want to marry you in front of everyone. All my brothers, your family. Everyone." He grinned his heart-stopping grin. "But we can start the honeymoon now."

"Really?"

"Oh hell yeah!"

He swept her up in his arms before he kicked the door shut with his boot. "Where's your bedroom?"

"Down the hall, cowboy."

"I'm gonna make you scream, city girl."

"Promise?"

"Promise with all my heart and soul."

Sandy Sullivan

Epilogue

The fire in the fireplace hissed from the gas logs. Rain pounded on the roof outside but Mesa didn't care. She sat wrapped safe and warm in her husband's arms while they lounged on the rug in front of the fireplace in nothing but bare skin. She had her very own happily ever after with her cowboy. Soft country music played over the stereo system. A little George Strait always put her in the mood for lovin'. Tonight was no exception. Of course, it was their wedding night. The honeymoon would commence the next day with a trip to Jamaica, but they'd decided to spend the night in their cabin.

After he'd shone up on her doorstep in Los Angeles, they'd spent the day and night making up for lost time. It only took one I love you to tell her she belonged with this man back in Texas. He went home after a week, leaving her there to settle her life, give up her apartment and pack a truck. He then flew back to ride from L.A. to Bandera with her. Their wedding took only three months to plan. She couldn't have waited much longer even though they loved the nights away in their little spot of heaven beneath the wide Texas night sky.

Noise coming from outside startled her out of her musings until she snuggled back down against him.

"Don't worry, darlin'." His kissed the top of her head. "It's just my brothers causing a ruckus."

"What are they up to?" She sat up and turned around in his arms. "They aren't like painting your truck with shaving cream or something, are they?"

"I don't know, but I'd expect them to tie cans to the back bumper. I ain't the first to get married since Jeff did it before me, but I'm the first to have my wife snuggled up next to me on our weddin' night here in my cabin. Jeff spent his wedding night alone."

"Seriously? What the hell?"

"I told you she was a bitch. She went out after the wedding with her friends, passed out on someone's floor and didn't come home until two days later."

"Wow." She glanced down at her wedding rings with a smile. "I can't believe we're married." A not so quick kiss to his lips forestalled her next words for several minutes. She loved kissing Joel, anytime, anywhere. They usually made the family uncomfortable with their show of affection. "It was a beautiful ceremony even though it rained."

"But it was great to have it in front of the fireplace in the main lodge." He pushed a piece of hair behind her ear before he trailed his fingertips along her jaw. "You looked beautiful in your dress. Did I tell you that?"

"You have now. You looked pretty handsome in your cowboy finery." She kissed his neck. "Did I ever tell you I have a thing for cowboys?"

"No really? I would never have guessed." He laughed.

She punched him in the side.

"Ow!"

"Oh, I did not hurt you."

He gave her a wounded look with a little pouty lip. Unable to resist, she leaned in and sucked his bottom lip between her teeth before she took a nip of it. A soft moan escaped his mouth as he grabbed her head, slanting it just so for a deeper kiss. Their tongues tangled for a good while before he lifted his head and looked into her soul with those beautiful blue eyes.

"I love you Mrs. Young."

"I love you too, Mr. Young. So much. More than anything in this life." Tears formed, spilling down her cheeks.

"Hey! Why the tears?"

"Happy tears. I'm so glad you came to L.A."

"You've already thanked my mother for her intervention on your behalf like a thousand times."

He tucked her in next to his side, holding her close. Her head rested on his broad chest. "I wouldn't know what to do if you hadn't."

"I'm beyond thrilled we don't have to find out. Now, hush. I have a wife to love."

"Hmm," she hummed in between kisses. "I like your thinking, Sir."

"Good. Kiss me, woman."

"Where, Sir?"

"Anywhere you want."

THE END

Secret Cravings Publishing
www.secretcravingspublishing.com

Made in the USA
Charleston, SC
15 March 2015